Smokes and Birds

James Simpson

Artwork by Bridget Murray

First published in 2021 by James Simpson,
Rushcroft Press, Derry

© James Simpson, 2021

ISBN: 978-1-3999-0069-0

Project management by Dingle Publishing Services

Design by Dennison Design

Printed by Walsh Colour Print

Printed in Ireland using paper from sustainable forest resources only

For Jen with love and gratitude

Acknowledgements

The love of writing stories comes, I believe, from my wonderful, imaginative mother, Norah. Self-belief I owe in large measure to the inspirational R. Irwin Knight, who affirmed me in his amazing English classes at Banbridge Academy. A heartfelt thank you goes to everyone who has helped me along my writing journey since then, including the judging panel of the Francis McManus Short Story Competition. Thank you, RTÉ for broadcasting my story, 'Dark Secret', and to Penguin Ireland for longlisting 'The Long Spoon'. I'm deeply indebted to the judges of the Irish Novel Fair, and to Colm Arbuckle who gave me the opportunity to read on Radio Ulster.

Special thanks to Bernie McGill who got me started at Flowerfield Arts Centre in Portstewart and who has always been such a generous fount of wisdom. Thanks to the many other authors whose workshops I have attended over the years, including Martina Devlin, Claire Kilroy and Felicity McCall. Thanks to the staff of the Irish Writers' Centre, Dublin, the XBorders: Transition team, the staff and fellow students of the Seamus Heaney Centre at Queen's University Belfast and in particular, Professor Ian Sansom. I deeply appreciate the nurturing given by members of North Coast Writers and This Writing Thing in Derry, for their constructive, critical expertise, especially Sue Divin, Maureen Dunseath, Mary Farrell, Geraldine Fleming and Robin Holmes. Thank you, Peter North, sadly missed, and Corrie Johnson for help with editing other work.

Thank you, Venie Martin and Christine O'Kane of Causeway and Foyle u3a branches for your interest in promoting my work. Thank you, Jenni Doherty for your early promise to stock the book in my local bookstore, Little Acorns. Thank you, Patrick McGill for years of patient IT support, and also James Cunningham.

Thank you, Derry City and Strabane District Council for your financial endorsement via the terrific Individual Artist Award scheme. Thank you, Hilda Quinn for being a faithful, perceptive and honest first reader. Thank you, Bridget Murray for the outstanding art work and John Boyle for suggesting and taking the photograph. And of course, thank you, Siobhán Prendergast and the team at Dingle Publishing, not least of all designer Tessa, who have been only magnificent.

Thank you, Jen for your love, care and advice, for putting up with me and for helping with ideas, alternatives, the final selection and editing of the stories.

James Simpson

Photo: John Boyle

James Simpson grew up in east Belfast. After a career in the Health Service, and helping to set up Oakgrove Integrated College, he graduated with distinction in Creative Writing from The Seamus Heaney Centre, QUB in 2019. A runner up in the Francis McManus Short Story Competition in 2013, he was subsequently longlisted for the RTÉ Guide/Penguin Short Story Competition and became an Irish Novel Fair finalist in 2019. His work has been published in *Blackbird*, *On the Grass When I Arrive*, and read on Radio Ulster and RTÉ. He was selected as a participant in the Irish Writers' Centre's XBorders: Transition Programme 2019. He has three children and two grandchildren, and lives with his wife, Jen, in Derry and Dunseverick, on the north Antrim coast. *Smokes and Birds* is financially assisted by Derry City and Strabane District Council, for which he is very grateful.

Contents

Penelope's Party

Today, on his tenth anniversary, in what I believe people are already calling, 'The Jazz Age,' I am lighting a beeswax candle in memory of my dear, late brother – a good Irishman and British soldier. Many in our new country will detect an oxymoron, and to them I say, 'Bad cess.' For Francis Gerald Barret, it was time that was out of joint.

Each year, on this day, I have wanted to speak without hindrance about our last night together, before he sailed for Suvla, but to date have lacked the courage. So much has changed – I now want to make amends, for life is short. Our mother died young and I have developed a sense of impermanence. Who can tell what lies ahead? Others may decide whether I am being wise. I do not much care.

What I can say is this, on the summer night in question, on that precipitous occasion, Penelope Pendlebury, our dearest friend, played bravely her grand piano. Misty-eyed, she sang deeply of balls and marble halls for the departing troops – and other less loyal friends, I had no doubt – assembled in her drawing room, climaxing perfectly in a blaze of chords.

'Nothing like romance, Penny,' said the banker, Jervis – she hated 'Penny' – helping himself to the Elviro Garcia. Then, lowering his voice, 'and where, if you don't mind me asking, is Ireland's leader on this fine night?'

'John Redmond could not join us,' she said, coolly, as though it did not matter, 'but we shall carry on.' This was to prove a blessing, I am sure, for Redmond. One wondered though, how Jervis knew to ask, for Redmond's appearance had naturally, not been advertised.

The officers, stiffly handsome and smelling war, were gallantry itself, and loving her desperately. True to her patriotic nature, Penelope wore a laurel spray of green. And this was as it should be, for then, I confess, I saw no ambiguity. But time, like the soldiers, has marched on.

'Quite so,' said Jervis, swirling his schooner, 'another time.'

'Oh, isn't it such a night though,' said Penelope, turning to me, grasping my hand with trembling fingers. Which may have been excitement.

Next, and without invitation, a tall, furtive-looking man, who had arrived on, of all things, a motorcycle, rendered a monologue. It concerned the murder of a landlord in Roscommon in the 1860s, and left me puzzled.

'How very unusual,' Penelope murmured, a frown flitting, before she clapped and said, 'I don't know who he is, poor chap.' Perhaps it had been portentous, for nothing was straightforward.

All this seems so long ago, but time is a mystery. I recall two harpers playing O'Carolan with willowy Gaelic fingers, plucking earnest strings thoughtfully, cradling their ancient instruments against flat chests. They also sang in Irish and received some polite applause.

And need I mention the deranged Medusa to their left, keening, complex tears flowing – for it was a trying time in one's native land. Her unlikely companion, the Major, was still my brother then. Where he had met her, or why, I never grasped. Needless to say, it was the most platonic of relationships, but he was good to her, as one might be to a wounded animal or a deranged bear whose claws had been torn out. And for all his reticence, let me tell you, he was as fine a patriot as any.

When a plump Signora brought her screeching aria to an end, the

Major said, 'Bravo,' in, I suppose, a colonial manner, but it was merely his way. Indeed, after no persuasion, he gave a passable 'Kathleen Mavourneen', in the tenor style of McCormack, which doubtless surprised a few.

And indeed, there were the others, whom Penelope, with her vast eclectic circle, had asked, as well as their friends and hangers on. All creeds and credos were welcome in her house. Men in spectacles huddled in corners, their heads together, brooding. Assertive women of the literary type conversed freely, a number of them unattached.

'Turks' and 'tomorrow', were not popular words. Not happy thoughts to inspire, at a troubled time. They spelled loss for some. For them cockcrow would be a clarion. For others, and I knew this well, a denial. Such was the unspoken tension of the times. Mercifully, the dawn was still some hours away.

So, Mr Redmond was missing out. Viands. My Lord. Penelope had left no stone, as they say, no stone: cold meats, glazed fruits, chocolate sourced from Belgium (some time ago, but excellent). Her trestle tables bore only the best wines and whiskeys galore. All Irish. No Scotch. No English gin. No one took offence that I could see, and certainly not the Major.

An illusionist from Dalkey performed some engaging tricks, deceiving with playing cards. 'Sleight of hand is like Home Rule,' said Jervis, well on his way with Penelope's booze. The trickster pulled lengths of string straight from his throat.

'Good glory,' said Mrs Arbuthnot, the apothecary's wife, to her cousin Freda Farrell, 'you'll miss your Pádraig, when he goes.'

Freda looked away. There had been serious rifts. The future would be twisted, I saw that clearly, but Penelope was a big, expansive person with such inclusive faith that all could be overcome, and it was her party.

A kind of stage had been erected and after we drank a strong rum punch, local children performed a nativity play – God bless them, unseasonal, as it was – on account of the sailing. Sadness was my overwhelming emotion for pregnant little Mary, and the eager lambs, the fresh faces of these boys who would take their leave. The Major, without question, must have felt the same, subject to the discipline of his profession.

In fairness, any possible flagging of spirits was wonderfully allayed by the fiddlers from Mrs O'Rahilly's Celtic music school – Penelope counted her a personal friend – and each was arrayed in emerald.

Well, my goodness. Out and in and out and in, 'The Waves of Troy' and all of that - '*Tory* please, let's get it right,' said the doctor, Hurley, who seldom raised his voice. Tonight though, his tone was curt. People were more alert. Yet, above the random fragrances of ladies, hung a pleasantly blue tobacco pall.

I remarked to Sally Shaw, a horrendously inhibited woman, how good it was to see everyone together. 'Do you think so?' was all she said.

'It takes all sorts,' I said, echoing Penelope's mantra. How naïve one could be. I longed for a companionable banner to unfurl, but what one wants and what one gets … I yearned for a valedictory evening to remember, whatever might lie ahead for Ireland and, however abhorrent this may sound, vaguely, for the empire. How strange all that sounds now. It was, in retrospect, a night of lavish ambiguity, to be stored in the closets of the mind, a tale to treasure when snow would fall.

Mrs Grosse, doubtless Teutonic by origin, though no one would be crass enough to say, floated like a dumpling amongst the guests, bobbing against this one and that – readers and writers mostly, I would have thought, associates of her husband who kept a kind of bookshop on the quay. There had been rumours, but I banished them.

And then, alas, despite Penelope's best efforts, the evening hesitated, for life is not predictable. Perhaps a singer sang too many verses. Or someone had uttered the dreadful name of Carson or mentioned Ulster. A child recited, 'The White Man's Burden', written for Queen Victoria. Some eyebrows arched.

The fabric had begun to tear. I wonder if you can recall such a tingling moment, the exact second when a night rang hollow, or a bell clanged out of tune. When a key stuck fast on middle C, or a crack first appeared on some ceramic surface. It is something scarcely definable, is it not, in evidence only at the corners of mouths, in the clearing of throats, in the rebelling twang of an instrument, which no one seemed to touch?

'Charge your glasses for the King,' proposed the Major, dutifully, at midnight. There he was, my older brother, whose honest heart was pure, raising his glass, and making an effort. In his soul, I knew, in the very end that he would have no king. He had hinted as much privately, but the toast was unavoidable. Penelope, for all her poise, appeared to shrink. The soldiers stood. Some of the others kept their seats. How divisive these things would become.

'Carry on,' said Penelope then, striking a rag tune, 'Maple Leaf', I believe it was. I thought it did not suit the mood, but what do they say about a vacuum? From a wilting flower, the petals fell. A group of mummers followed, but seemed all out of sorts and stopped abruptly.

'A feast or a famine,' said the Major, glancing with some relief, at our father's Half Hunter watch.

'That's hardly the sort of language for an Irish soirée,' said Hurley, who had scarcely drunk a thing.

'Hear, hear,' crooned the unsteady Jervis,

'What isn't?' said the Major, rounding on them. I could see the fleck of spittle on his lip.

'Your allusion to the Famine,' said Hurley. 'A million dead, a million fled. Your mention of it, sir, is trite.'

'Good God in heaven,' said the Major. His eye had begun to twitch, like when he was a boy. His fists had clenched. 'Let us first despatch the bloody Hun and his pals,' he said, 'and then…' Then what? In that instant, I pictured him, pistol in hand, leading a charge to capture some stupid hill. But afterwards, I wondered.

We found the Medusa deep in conversation with Mrs Grosse and two unsmiling youths, intense Fáinne wearers and scholars by the look of them. Poor poets maybe. The sort who argued late at night and looked quite down at heel.

'Come,' said the Medusa, 'meet Mr Connolly and Mr Devlin, who have been to America no less, and speak my language. They have no time for Redmond. They see a better way.'

The Major – whose impeccable manners I can vouch for as his sister – did not stretch out a hand.

'And so, tomorrow you sail,' said one of the youths, who were older than they looked. He proffered a cigarette, which was instantly declined. 'I hope that you have luck.'

One does not mistake false notes.

'Luck. Do you now, do you really?' said the Major, who was quick to read a man. He straightened his jacket. His face was crimson. I trembled, fearing violence. 'There's more than the likes of you and your comrades that wants a change in Ireland,' he said. 'Just give us a bloody chance, God damn you.'

The Medusa stopped her ears. The poets shrugged, at ease with Frau Grosse.

'You'll see,' they said, 'you'll see.'

'You're not thinking of leaving already, Francis?' Penelope shimmered like the perfect hostess. She had donned her stole, though I found myself perspiring.

'It's been awfully good of you,' the Major said, recovering quickly – I loved him in that moment – 'but I rather think…'

'He's dragging me off,' the Medusa said, in an amazing, intuitive way. 'Well, goodbye, lads.'

'Go on, Major, if you must,' said Penelope, weighing it up. Balancing, feeling perhaps, that some things had, after all, been too much, that she had tried too hard to square a suspect circle.

'*Slán*,' said the Medusa, bowing to the poets.

It was then I noticed again the solitary figure of the motorcyclist and thought how sinister he seemed, though no one had been killed. Not Redmond, thankfully, for the notion had crossed my mind.

The Major clicked his heels. An alien thing, I thought. Frau Grosse saluted a farewell. Obscenely, I would recall her mocking gesture, weeks later when I came to read the telegram.

DREW ENEMY FIRE STOP SHELL STOP MADE
GOOD CONFESSION STOP

Stop, stop, stop. Words, words, staccato as bullets. So, a priest had been with him.

As the curtain fell on Penelope's party, the Major kissed her and me on both our cheeks and, enigmatic man that he was, simply bore the Medusa away.

Penelope sighed. 'We are a convoluted people, are we not?' she said, flinging her arms aloft, like Moses on the mountain, still reaching for what we came to know as 'The impossible'. 'Bon voyage,' she said, 'to you, and you and also you. Please God there will be room for us all when William and Seamus return in the gloaming.' It was a lot to ask. And it wasn't to be.

The young men swore. I thought them arrogant, but they saw how it would go, though not the whole picture, admittedly; not all the terrible beauty that would be born. How could they, for no one is clairvoyant. That lies with God.

I took Penelope's arm. I gasped at how fragile it seemed. I said, 'Don't worry, my pet. Don't worry darling. What a splendid evening. All will be fine. Yes, all will be well.'

The Spider and the Fly

On the Friday night before Ulster Day, Sammy McClure, carpenter, husband and father of Maggie, left McLister Street, again, to walk the two miles home. The street was nothing new. But his visits had stayed sweet, for she had become his compulsion. The one person who understood what he was up against. Beckie kept him going from week to week, and she was a secret. When he wasn't with her, he was thinking about her. She flushed him with warmth. When he dreamed, he dreamed of Number 4, where it was calm and soft, and he could be himself. Every step away from her was a step in the wrong direction but he had to do it.

At the end of each shipyard week, he went there, after the horn. It was a great thing to do, but not a good or a wise thing. To hell. On this late September evening his route was, as ever, full of men in flat caps pedalling black bicycles, but it was also wild with Union flags, and vibrating with loyal tunes. Toothy flutes whistled for tomorrow and young fellas marched with sticks because Ulster would fight Home Rule, and Ulster would be right. All that was a big mistake, according to Sammy, who knew his own mind. His smile lapsed with every pace he took, till it evaporated altogether, somewhere about the junction with the big road.

He kept his soul in McLister Street, but his body was forced to live with Peg. To death do us part, but Peg was tubercular, and Maggie who looked after her was a saint. Belfast was full of bloody saints.

Maggie would have the pigs' liver waiting for him – a reproach – simmering on a pure bed of onions, glistening and stewing in the pan. And he would lie to her, as usual, for he was the man who could roll out fabrications. And use his fists, if he needed to, in his own house, when black anger was on him. Stupidity in others made him impatient. So did this cursed Covenant, and the half loaf of life that was supposed to be better than no bread. Maggie's solicitude was getting to him.

He crossed the tramlines, which the world and its uncle would follow tomorrow on their way to sign. He was damned if he would stand like a fool at the City Hall, with the sheep. But he wasn't dumb. He knew what people said. 'There's McClure. A good joiner, but is he sound?' Because you had to be sound. When you were sound you didn't argue. You went along. You always did. You said, 'Yes.' Then your mates could count on you, if it ever came to the bit. And it might. It could.

But Sammy was his own man and nobody would tell him what to think. This was the sort of stuff that spiralled through his head when he lay down alone, at night to sleep, and thought of Beckie, in the wee back room.

He smelled the liver the minute he opened the door. The fresh bread as well. 'How's your mammy?' he said to Maggie, like he was asking for a stranger. He didn't look near her, as he threw off the jacket, and shoved his lunch box in her face.

Peg hadn't cooked for years. She'd never been strong. Maybe he'd never wanted her. Once a woman took to her bed, you were up shit creek. So, he'd looked elsewhere.

'Fridays are a long day for you, Father,' Maggie bleated, the way he hated. Her sleeves were well pulled up to drain the spuds. And to let him see the bruise on her arm, where he'd caught her.

'I told you about that,' he said. It was annoying to look at. For him to see what he had done. She paraded it and it offended him. Made him think he was some sort of beast. She liked displaying it. Having it noticed. Trotting out her own little sacrament. He'd said nothing about it in McLister Street. God it was easy to smile there.

'It's all right, Daddy,' Maggie said, treating him like a fool. 'I knocked it on the shelf.' He couldn't stand a doormat. 'Well, cover it up,' he said. 'It's turning my stomach.'

He seldom looked at himself. Only when he shaved in the mornings. Then he saw the grim face of life belly up. He was sure that he hadn't always been like this. But the infection in his soul had grown, and now it was visible. Nothing was adding up. Love or lust was taking its toll. The life force was draining out of him, as well as Peg. He couldn't stop it and he wouldn't. But how could something so beautiful appear so ugly?

Maggie had set his place. He would eat alone, with his thoughts. She brought him buttermilk in a beaker, cold, the way he liked it. He lashed it down his throat. Relishing the sourness.

'How was oul Robbie the day?' she asked, like the wee woman she was in her apron mashing turnip.

He had invented Robbie.

Ach, he's not great now,' he said, rubbing his eyes, 'he's worse than your mother. He's not the man I worked with, poor divil never sees a soul.'

'Except you, every Friday,' she said fussing over the pot. Would she give his head peace? 'Did you see much stir?'

'What? Oh aye, plenty,' he said, letting on to be civil. 'I'll eat this here before I go up to her.' Peg was a coughing machine.

'Give us another drop would you?' he said. The beaker was at his mouth when they heard the knock. Now who the hell was that? He looked at Maggie, hating that nervous, startled thing she did. She'd got it from Peg. 'Are you not going to see who it is?'

'It's not Thursday,' she said, 'so it isn't the rent man.'

'Aye, well, it's somebody, isn't it? Just answer the bloody door.' He sliced the liver into tight little strips. Shovelled on salt. Listened for the rasp of the weatherboard. He'd have to sand it. She was talking to somebody. Where was the pepper? 'Come in,' she was saying. He shook the brown sauce bottle. It came in a splurge. If some fella was calling on her, by God he'd hammer him. A man's shoes scuffled. A familiar voice.

'Oh yes,' Maggie was saying, all proper, 'he's only in the door. He's at his dinner, but sure, come in. Would you eat a bit of soda? Oh, Father,' she said, like she was announcing Asquith, 'it's Mr Irvine, your boss from your work.'

Bumper Irvine. This was a first. But not a good first. Bumper wedged his head into the kitchen.

'Evening, Sammy,' he said. 'I'm disturbing you. The summer is well advanced.'

Advanced? The summer? What summer? 'What's the story, Bumper?'

'The nights are closing in,' said Bumper. What was this here?

Bumper was a scrappy joiner. The only reason he got to be a foreman was the Masons, so he had pull. He was the sort of foreman that asked you to explain a drawing to him after he'd handed it to you. But his voice was loud and convincing. He wore a phoney waxed moustache, and a hat on weekdays, and he reached his umbrella to Maggie. 'Don't let me leave without it, darling,' he said, 'in case I get distracted.' He set the hat on the kitchen table, finding a spot that was close to Sammy's dinner. 'Don't splash it now,' he said.

'You'll sit down, Mr Irvine?' Maggie said.

Bumper was already making himself at home, pulling out a chair, and lowering his bulk. He sat dead opposite Sammy, and sighed. 'How's the missus?' he asked, as if he cared. Sammy looked at the liver, seeing it for what it was. The hunger was off him. It was offal. And this was no social call.

Bumper was starched up in his Sunday best, but he loosened the top button of his waistcoat and looked about him, taking in the room like he was going to buy the place. There wasn't much to see. Maggie's stitched sampler on the wall, 'Mother and Home'. Two china dogs. One chipped. A faded picture of a highland cow. 'You have a nice wee set up here, Sammy, so you do,' he said, smirking at the bareness. 'Very clean and comfortable. A dry, happy home is a boon, I say, a boon.'

Sammy edged his plate away, avoiding the hat.

'Don't stop eating on my account,' Bumper said, smiling at his loss of appetite. 'Maggie here will pour me a cup of tea, won't you, pet? Four sugars, and one of your farls would go a long way. One with a nice brown bottom.' He gazed at Maggie. 'What age are you now, daughter?'

'Fifteen,' she said.

'Fifteen,' he sighed again. 'Perfect with a knob of butter, what do you say, Sammy?'

'There's a taste of jam for you,' Maggie said. 'I'm away up to Mammy.'

'God bless you,' Bumper said, taking a good look at her arm. 'You're late at your dinner, pal,' he said to Sammy.

Best say nothing.

'She's a great wee blade, all the same,' Bumper said, sucking his tea. 'What would we do without the women, eh? You're a lucky man, to have a stand in.'

Sammy's mouth was dry.

Bumper wiped the bristles of his moustache with a pressed handkerchief and belched as he leaned into Sammy's space. 'I don't need to tell you,' he said, 'there's a lot going on, one way and another, out there.' He took a long swallow of tea, and yanked his thumb in the direction of the street.

Sammy waited.

'To tell you the truth,' said Bumper, like he was talking to his brother, 'I've never seen so many good people milling about. All getting ready. Such a sense of purpose. You can actually feel it. D'ye know what I'm saying?'

Sammy knew what he was saying.

'Tomorrow's the day,' said Bumper, choosing his words. 'It's all over the *Telegraph*. You won't have had time to read it, being only in and all. Oh, aye, "Day of Destiny".' He leaned back on the hard chair, making it balance it on two rigid legs. There was poor light in the room. His florid face was in shadow now. For a minute Sammy couldn't see the evil in his eyes.

'The boys, of course,' said Bumper, 'are solid to a man, except for the Short Strand mob, but then, we'd hardly expect the fenians to sign "The Solemn League and Covenant" now would we?' He laughed at that. 'That would be some geg. But wait till I tell you, McClure, a quarter of a million good Protestant men will pledge themselves.' His face had darkened. 'Are you listening to me, Sammy? And, Carson, yes Carson will be there. I suppose you've heard of him?' He was enjoying this. 'You wouldn't miss it now, would you?' Bumper reached forward, and gripped Sammy's shoulder. 'You'll want your name on the roll of honour? Won't you, son?' He was younger than Sammy.

There was no sign of Maggie. Bumper lifted the enamel teapot and swirled it round. 'Plenty left for another cup,' he said, walloping it down again on the range. Then he paused. Timing was important.

'You're very quiet, Sammy,' he said. 'I'm not making a big thing of it, you know. I don't want you to take it the wrong way. The boys just wanted me to make sure you weren't worrying about your daughter there, or the wife, God love them. Her being took bad and all.'

Sammy opened a window.

'Not that it's affected your work,' said Bumper. 'Do you know what I think? I think you're no mug. You're a... clever fella. No, I mean it.' He had hesitated for a second. It was long enough. This was some performance. 'But you need more than brains in this game,' he said, running a dry palm over his skull. 'This here's all about sol-id-ar-ity.' The word broke in his mouth. 'Are you with me, Sammy? You do understand? There really will be no pope here.'

'Can I get Mammy a drink of water?' Maggie whispered, opening the kitchen door a crack. Her eyes narrowed. 'Oh glory,' she said, 'I didn't mean to disturb youse. Did you like the bread Mr Irvine?'

'I loved it, sweetheart,' said Bumper. 'The man that gets you will be in clover, I say, in clover. Powerful wee girl,' he said, his eyes following her.

Sammy wished that Maggie hated him. She was too good. Hate would have been easier.

'I'll put it to you this way,' Bumper said, 'the men are jumpy. You know yourself. Very jumpy. I know, for instance, that you eat your piece with the boul Sean Quinn. Now that, Sammy, under the circumstances, is not the behaviour of a wise man. Not these days with feelings running. It's like in boxing, you have to look out for the long reach. Are you with me? I'm trying to help you, because I like you.' He jabbed a finger in his ear and wiggled it. 'She's a handy wee baker, too,' he said. 'Have you any fegs on you?'

Sammy passed him his pack of Players.

'If it was up to me,' Bumper said, 'I'd cut you a bit of slack, honest to God, I would, on account of your old mother being a Catholic.'

This was a hard punch.

'Who told you my mother –' But Bumper cut him off. 'See when you're a foreman, you're looking at the whole man, warts and all. You need to know everything about him. I would say nothing, if it was up to me. But it's not up to me, Sammy, is it? It's up to you. What way are you going to jump tomorrow?' Bumper's teeth were long. He had eaten a lot of men. Well, let him bloody salivate. 'You see,' Bumper said, 'there's a rumour going about that you're agin it. God, the very thought of it.' He looked away, like he wanted a cheer for saying something filthy.

Sammy was a suspect in his own house. He didn't feel like smoking. Upstairs Peg was choking away. Maggie would be plumping her pillow. Cooing at her like a pigeon. Praying like a nun. 'You're going to be fine, Mammy. God will raise you up.'

Bumper cracked his knuckles. 'Awk aye, I know you've a lot to contend with, Sammy, so tell your uncle Bumper that there's no need to worry.' He tapped his hat. 'Do you like it? I bought it for tomorrow.'

Sammy knew he was supposed to speak. To make his case. To defend himself, but why should he explain what he thought about Ireland to a shite like Irvine? Why should he tell him that having a Catholic ma was nothing to do with it? That he'd worked it out for himself?'

'What about choice?' was all he said, and he knew it was too much.

'I'm all for choice,' said Bumper, 'and so are the men – as long as you make the right decision. Ulster will fight…'

'I know all that,' Sammy said. 'God save the King and to hell with His Nibs. The next thing youse will be bringing out guns.'

'You better believe it,' said Bumper, 'we will if we have to, and then where will you be? But like I say, that's not up to you or me.'

Bumper was the spider and Sammy was getting the legs pulled off him. Bumper was on his feet now. He was going to the yard. 'The more tea, the more you pee.'

He had underestimated him. This was their big chance to flush him out. To tar him as a Shinner. He wasn't a big man. Not a brave man. God knows he wasn't even an honest man. But he wasn't without principle altogether. Here was a chance to take a stand.

The latch clicked. Bumper was back, filling a basin, rubbing his hands with the Lifebuoy in the jawbox. 'I like your pink geraniums out there,' he said, 'they're lasting well. Where's your towel, Sammy boy? Oh aye, I see it now. Did you make the roller yourself? I suppose your missus is never down the stairs at all? Youse have a hard oul station too.'

'We're doing all right,' said Sammy.

'Of course you are.' Bumper, stood with his back to the range, scorching his backside, and loving it. 'And you want to keep it that way.' Outside the drums were pounding.

'In a hundred years they'll still be talking about it, you know,' said Bumper.

'This Covenant will divide the country,' said Sammy. 'We'll never get rid of it.'

But Bumper wasn't listening. 'That there's the most magical music in the world,' he said, taking out his silver cigarette case. He plucked one of his own. Snapped shut the case. No feg for Sammy. 'Have you seen the light?' asked Bumper, dragging smoke through his lungs.

'I'm not going to do it,' Sammy said. 'Ireland will be better under Dublin in the long run. I've always thought that.'

'Oh Sammy, Sammy.' Bumper was shaking his big boxer's head, like he'd heard a joke. The blattering got louder.

'It's funny, all the same,' said Bumper, 'how the road home's always longer on a Friday evening. Did you ever notice that?' His eyes were moist with feeling. 'I get back at the house for six myself. But it must be great to dander along and watch the world go by. And take your time.'

Upstairs, Peg was bringing up phlegm.

'Maybe she could be doing with you,' said Bumper, 'maybe loving her's not enough.' He was on to him. He was taking him apart. 'Aye, Friday night is detour night,' he said, 'are you keeping up?'

Sammy worked at a skelf in his thumb.

'You know as well as I do,' said Bumper, 'how sensitive the fairer sex can be. Small things annoy them. My woman's the same. They hear a groundless rumour and they start the blubbing. It's in their nature. Us men… now we wouldn't for the world… you know what I'm saying. That's a sore-looking thumb.'

Sammy had cornered rats. He knew the look in their eyes before he slammed them with a lump of wood.

'I like McLister Street, myself,' said Bumper, out of nowhere. 'Lovely wee houses. Fancy brick porches, tidy parlours. Every damned thing in them a man could want.' He took a long, slow pull. 'Do you mind Jack Dobbins? Sure, I know you do. The fella that fell off the scaffold. Terrible tragedy. Good on fine work, but he did stupid things. He got careless. Had a lot of friends that were taigs, and his plank gave way.'

'He had no time for Craig and his pals, that's what,' said Sammy.

'No, that's what I'm saying,' said Bumper, 'God knows how his widow is paying her bills now. What's this her name was? They lived in McLister Street. A woman like that could be lonely, so she could. They have their needs as well. Maybe when Peg gets better the two of them could get together, like, and be a bit of company for each other.'

Bumper lifted the china dog without the chip. He passed it from hand to hand. 'It wouldn't do to drop it,' he said, placing it beside his hat.

The spider had the last leg off. The fly was still wriggling.

Maggie was down for the stone hot water bottle. 'She's asking for you, Daddy.'

'There you are,' said Bumper. 'I told you. I'm holding you back.'

'Is there anything wrong?' Maggie asked.

'What the hell would be wrong?' said Sammy. She did her shrinking act.

'There's not a thing the matter, Maggie,' said Bumper, 'that a cuddle wouldn't fix.' He studied her pale pinched face. 'Your daddy here and I were just speaking about a wee problem we have at Harland's. Men's talk, that's all. We've studied it up and down, like you have to in the shipyard.'

'Did you find the answer?' she asked.

'Oh, I think so,' said Bumper. 'We always get there in the end, so don't be annoying yourself. But, I say, that's a bad-looking burn on your arm,' he was looking at Sammy.

'It was my fault, Mr Irvine,' said Maggie, 'I'm always doing it on the kettle, it's nothing. She wants you Daddy,' she said.

'Shite, I know,' said Sammy.

'Language,' said Bumper, pulling out his watch. Eyeing his hat, checking it for japs. 'It's time I wasn't here. Elsie will be thinking I'm away with another woman, and that would never do, would it, Maggie? Now what were you going to fetch me, pet?'

'Oh mercy,' said Maggie, 'your umbrella.'

Bumper held up her arm. He shook his head at Sammy. 'Now that there's none of my business,' he said, 'but you should be ashamed.'

'Here's your brolly,' said Maggie. 'I'm forgetting Mammy's jar.'

'You're a good girl,' Bumper said pressing a sixpence into her hand. 'Whatever you say, say nothing, eh.' His finger was at his lip. 'I hope your daddy's good to you. The boys will be waiting for him at nine in the morning, at the corner of May Street. Don't be letting him sleep in. It wouldn't do for him to miss signing the Covenant.'

'But he's not going to sign it, Mr Irvine, are you, Daddy?' she said, opening the door.

'Let's put it this way,' Bumper said, 'it's not a weakness to change your mind.'

They stood, waiting for Bumper to adjust his hat. Then when he looked the part, they were in the street. A crowd of wee girls were skipping, using one big rope, jigging and dancing and waiting to get in.

'Lord, would you listen to them innocent creatures,' said Bumper, as the girls sang:

> *My aunt Jane, she's awful smart*
> *She bakes wee rings in an apple tart*
> *And when Halloween comes round*
> *Fornenst that tart I'm always found.*

Beckie was no tart.

'That's one for you, big lad,' said Bumper, thumping Sammy on the back. 'Could you credit that? Boys, you'd swear they know. They're not a bit slow.' The drummers drummed on.

It was no contest.

'Ah now,' said Bumper, glancing at the sky, 'we've all a lot to be thankful for, so we have.' He grasped Sammy's hand. 'You've made the right call anyway,' he said, pumping hard. 'You know that yourself. There'll be no more bother now. Now that we're all pulling together, there won't be a word about it. But see and get your daddy to do something about that arm,' he said to Maggie. 'You're a great girl, so you are, and a lovely girl. What do you say, Sammy? Am I right or am I wrong?'

Glimmering Lights

Andrew Whalley was an immaculate, hard man. Each weekday morning, at six I placed a copy of the *Times* and the *Belfast News-Letter* on his breakfast tray and took it to his study. At five minutes past seven, I drove him to his mill in the Chambers car. His workers were by then well into their shift.

'Driving is not for me, Rodgers,' he often said. 'Not while I can afford a well-paid chauffeur.' In fact, he paid me very little. But I stuck with him.

I wore goggles and a cap, but he refused both, thrusting his impregnable old body into the passenger seat beside me, where he would talk without a break – of linen, money and himself. He had started in Alderdice's at the age of thirteen and from the beginning was, 'fascinated by linen. Its strength and versatility. I can't turn it out fast enough,' he said. 'You can make anything at all out of linen, from kitbags to aircraft. The war is an absolute boon, if you're in the right industry.' And he knew he was.

Whalley had served his time as a fitter. 'I never approached a seasoned man for advice before I used my own brain,' he said. 'It let them see the wise head I had on me. When it was time to go home, I was the last to leave. Cultivating my reputation, Rodgers,' he said.

I heard all this more times than 'The Lord's Prayer'. He had no interest in battles or of men being slaughtered in France.

One evening, Mr Alderdice had asked his opinion on 'a production matter'. Now that was a red-letter day in Whalley's life. 'Carnage is an awful thing Rodgers,' he said, 'but, think about it, men can be replaced in time, whereas, commerce is the lifeblood of any country.' Boot straps were the answer; pulling yourself up, but without commotion or wearing your heart on your sleeve. Going to bed early, plain food, abstinence and knowing your place was the Ulster way. There would be plenty of time for plucking harps in the next life.

A lot of men were doing that already, thanks to the Germans. I was not going to volunteer. I stayed in Ulster, where I was.

Whalley told me that he'd made himself indispensable to Mr Alderdice, who gave him his chance in the office, and that's where he'd learned the trade, bottom to top. Eventually he was allowed to attend meetings with bankers and other manufacturers but he'd 'never got ideas above his station.'

And so, as war ebbed and blood flowed in the mud of Europe, I listened to him on our daily drives to the mill and formed my own opinions.

Mr Alderdice's wife took a shine to him. She and her husband had no heir. Whalley showed her 'understanding,' he said, which she found endearing. One day, at the turn of the century, she'd asked him for tea. A great honour. This was to be the first of many invitations. He also accepted the 'stiff and formal' suits she bought for him, as his own rough clothes were 'a label of poverty, to be frank'. He felt her warming to him in 'a motherly way'.

'Of course, Rodgers,' he said, 'I don't need to tell you that I never referred to any of that in the mill. I'm relying on you, to observe the same diplomacy.'

I must admit I smiled. Occasionally, on our journeys, he would tut at a badly parked milk cart or a limping bicycle on the road, but this was more for punctuation than anything, and in general, he was relaxed, as we sailed between the hedges. 'I was blessed with wisdom beyond my years,' he said. 'You should cultivate that same attribute.' I told him that I would try.

The Alderdices told him that he had a future. 'It was such a relief,' he said, 'to be away from my parents' impoverished warren. I may as well tell you,' he said, one morning, when the news from France was particularly grim, 'that although I was no longer on the mill floor every day, I noted the grumblers and slackers and reported them to Mr Alderdice.'

Soon, he was attending gatherings of industrialists where there was much debate. He learned the power of argument and weighed up the opposition. He was blessed with photographic recollection and, 'Mr A', as he called him, was greatly taken with his acumen.

It was at one of these meeting that he met a certain George Sewell, of Woods and Woods, their chief competitor. As the proceedings ended, Sewell, it seemed, had suggested refreshments at a coffee house in Cornmarket.

'My natural inclination, as you can imagine, Rodgers, was to say no,' he said, 'but I thought I might learn something to advantage. You will find that people are seldom what they appear. Sewell seemed to be a jolly chap, but I knew he had no real interest in the trade and was fond of gambling. I would not have been surprised to find him at a cock fight. Necessity forced him to show his hand, and he took a chance, Rodgers.'

I remember so well Whalley telling me that, as I eased the Chambers around a herd of cattle being chased by a mad fellow on a crutch, probably some shell-shocked soldier.

'It was apparent,' he said, 'that Sewell was stealing from his firm by selling second-quality cloth at half price, to his private "customers". He had been at this under-the-counter thievery for years. Are you listening, Rodgers?'

'I am, Mr Whalley,' I said, 'keeping my eye on the beasts.'

'He suggested that we work together,' said Whalley, 'to multiply profits. He was in debt, you see. But here's the thing, Rodgers,' he said, leaning so close across me, that I had to swerve, 'up to that point, I had not met dishonesty on any organised scale, but I did not protest. I refused to appear a prig.'

'That showed a lot of gumption, Mr Whalley,' I said, telling him what he wanted to hear. Echoing his own words, though I didn't like to talk and drive.

'You see,' he said, 'here were useful possibilities. So, I showed interest, which may surprise you, Rodgers. We agreed to meet in a week, in a different place, at night.'

We mostly travelled with the hood down. In God's fresh air. Sometimes I didn't catch all that Mr Whalley said, because of the wind, but I got every syllable of what he told me next. 'When I met Sewell in "The Pottinger",' he said, 'he had been drinking. Celebrating, like a fool, some surprise win. I told him that I was game. For the partnership.'

I drove on.

'Ho ho,' he said, 'I see that you are shocked, Rodgers, you weren't expecting that.'

I kept my eyes on the road.

'Sewell had already secured a number of extra orders,' he said. 'We agreed cash on delivery by a reliable man. I told him I had someone in mind but that it could take some weeks to organise. You see how important the details are?'

Whatever I thought about Whalley, he could certainly tell a story.

'I prepared a book for trading,' he said, 'and drew up an inventory for Sewell of the available seconds for him to share with clients. I made up a sample book so that the weights and densities could be fully appreciated.'

This was more than I needed.

'Don't let me distract you, Rodgers,' he said as I rounded the corner and saw the upright chimney of the mill. I slowed the Chambers to a crawl and parked her carefully, like I always did, but Whalley had not finished. He had to complete his tale. I eased on the brake and turned her off.

'I met Sewell as arranged,' he said. 'We climbed the stairs of a certain public house to the first floor where I picked a booth for privacy. Sewell was highly taken with my documentation. Thoroughness, as you know, is my middle name. "I know you enjoy a flutter," I said, "but I do not rely on chance." Are you paying attention to me, Rodgers?'

'I am, Mr Whalley.'

'Indeed. Exactly,' he said, with more excitement than I'd seen down through the years. 'Do you know what he said?' asked Whalley. 'He said, "My heart, your head." My head. Do you like that, Rodgers? Are you following my train of thought?'

He could hardly conceal his glee.

'"I knew you were a sound fellow," says he to me, and I said that he was on the money. Those were my very words.'

'And what did he say, Mr Whalley?'

'He slapped my back and offered me a cigar,' said Whalley. 'Now what do you think of that?' Inviting me to puff away profits before we had made a penny.'

'I don't know what to say, Mr Whalley,' I said, 'and that's a fact.'

'You see,' said Whalley, 'I had entered the spirit of the moment and believe it or not I ordered a decanter of claret and asked for an extra glass.'

'Now that *is* hard to credit,' I said.

Whalley beamed. 'You see, you see,' he said, 'I have your attention now. "Oh, you have hidden depths," he said to me, "hidden depths. And to hell with caution." Forgive my French. I asked the girl for another glass. "Are we expecting company?" laughed Sewell. "We are," I said, "bedad and we are."'

Whalley inflated like a toad. I snapped off my goggles and wondered what was coming. 'Sewell looked mystified,' he said. 'I knocked on the wall between us and the adjacent booth. Then Mr Alderdice appeared and joined us at the table, and he said, "This must be the young gentleman of whom you spoke, Whalley."'

Whalley's eyes were dancing now. He was stroking his moustache with pleasure. 'I need hardly tell you that Sewell's face had drained,' he said. 'He knew that he'd been nabbed. When the waitress returned, I poured three measures of claret. Then, despite my pledge never to touch strong drink, I proposed a toast, "To honesty in business," I said. Of course, Woods and Woods had been lax. I would have had a man like Sewell rumbled after a week.'

Whalley chuckled at the memory. 'Now, Rodgers, tell me,' he said, 'what do you make of that? Would that not beat any foolish picture you'd see in some cheap flicker palace? Is that not a saga and a half? We skinned him good and proper.'

'What happened to him?' I asked.

'Oh, he went down,' he said. 'You see, his mistake was to underestimate the cleverer man. That's how wars are lost.'

'Indeed it is,' I said.

'But what was my purpose, Rodgers,' he said, 'in telling all this to my humble chauffeur, at the risk of distracting his attention and damaging my precious Chambers? Was it to show him that I am impervious to corruption? Perhaps. Have I demonstrated the just deserts of a flawed human being, a worthless specimen? Or would you say that I'm flaunting a talent for intrigue?'

'I'm really not sure, Mr Whalley,' I said. 'That's all above my head.'

'Quite so,' he said. 'Quite so. Then I will tell you. Sewell's plan was robbery and the corruption of another man, but he didn't know his man, now, did he? Just think about it. I exposed a criminal in a neighbouring firm. I had, into the bargain, brought credit to Mr Alderdice by doing a good turn to his competitor, which cost him nothing, and enhanced his reputation. But above all, I like to think that I demonstrated the key quality, which all employers treasure beyond all others and that, as you know, Rodgers, is what?'

'Oh, loyalty wins hands down, Mr Whalley,' I said. 'Without a doubt.'

'It will hardly surprise you then,' he said, 'that the following year, Mr and Mrs Alderdice decided to leave the entire linen business to me. And that, Rodgers, is exactly what happened, with remarkable speed, when they passed away within a year of each other.'

'It's a great tale,' I said.

'Oh, it is, Rodgers,' he said. 'Some people will say it was luck. But I say, balderdash. Where would I be today, if I had relied on luck? Don't think it for a second. You need a good nose and a long head in commerce. And don't forget that linen has stood to us during this war, but now that it's ending we have to make a tapestry of the future. We have to turn to practicalities. To prepare for the next part of our journey. Make sure to give the Chambers a good wash down. Inspect her paintwork, and check her below, for the roads are a pure disgrace. Make sure you fill her to the neck.'

'Righto, Mr Whalley,' I said, peeling off my driving gauntlets and watching him walk the path through the wrought iron gate into his mill, with its dependable brick walls and predictable slate roof. I knew his keen eyes were sweeping his empire, in case he would miss a trick. His life had been one long production line. He had never stopped working, even if the mill was shut on a Sunday. He told me once that he'd spent Christmas Day reading financial reports. I had never heard of callers at his house. He had no interest in gardening or in going out at all. 'Who will get the mill,' I asked the maid, 'when he goes?'

'God knows,' she said.

He had never mentioned a family on our commute. He was opposed to philanthropy. 'You get nothing for nothing in my book,' he said. He resisted several requests, I believe, to sit on the board of the new technical college. In all the years I worked for him, I'd never met a tighter man.

I put the Chambers into gear and set off to buy fuel. There had been rows in Parliament about rationing petrol, but he had managed to get a good allocation under the scheme. We dealt with the Cochranes of the local hotel, who supplied petroleum spirit in red tins. He had given me strict instructions to make sure the lead seals were intact, to guard against cheating by providers palming off adulterated petrol, a practice widely reported by the papers. I knew the staff well and would be glad, as usual, of a hot cup of tea after the run.

We had a happy arrangement, which suited both of us. I signed for the cans. If they provided two tins, they wrote down three for me. If it was three, they wrote down four. It was an excellent system; we split the return on the additional gallon. They would give me an extra empty in case he asked, so there was no worry about tallying up. I enjoyed some good times with the cook there, too, a married woman called Brenda with a lot of energy. I had played my hunch. He checked the amount of petrol used against the price but his head was too stuffed with figures and calculations to ever ask how many miles the Chambers did to the gallon so he stayed oblivious. It was a dawdle, when I think of it now, all those trips I made to the post office, to lodge the buckshee cash.

I left Ireland after the war, while the going was good. Before I would push my luck. The day before I sailed, with my nest egg in a Gladstone bag, he gave me a small gift. When he'd bought the car, the manufacturers had enclosed an extra manual in error. It was 'carelessness,' he said, so he didn't hesitate to keep it. He 'very much,' wanted me to have it, as he knew I had treasured the car almost as much as he did. I assured him that I had learned a great deal about life from him, and had benefited more than he could ever know from my time in his service. I would be hard-pressed, I said, to find another such trusted position. He allowed himself a smile.

I would smile later, when I stood on the deck of the *Patriotic*, as it ploughed the lough on its way to Liverpool and the woman I had there, cutting through choppy waters, widening the distance between me and Mr Whalley, and the glimmering lights of Belfast.

One Cut

When they found her, the papers said, she wore one glove. Some animal, a badger, perhaps, had gnawed her other hand, the people said. This was rightly contested by the coroner who confirmed that it had been severed. 'Sliced' was the word he used.

Arabella was a funny girl. In the sense of 'strange'. I might have called her 'fey'. Her whitewashed house stood starkly in the picture, snapped by someone – I wonder who – that naïve spring evening, high on the upper mountain, but in a depression and out of sight. We all posed together in her sheep-stripped garden of sorts, thirteen young women linking arms in two smart rows, half smiling through instantly frozen lips.

Our brave beaux were fighting at the front, feet rotting, I supposed, in the rat runs of Kitchener's moustachioed panto. Squaring up to the wire and the Boche. Back in Ireland we shivered glamorously in summer dresses, with daring necklines, heads scandalously hatless. The photograph would become a bleak memorial, principally to Arabella, whose eighteenth birthday I assure you it was, and who would be lost on that tragic night forever. And how?

Look carefully. Study the grainy moment captured, perhaps with prescience, and in those faces you may divine the mystery for yourself.

Imagine the balm of June elsewhere that year. Bees buzzing, bleary with nectar. Yet, chilly winds were never far away in the hollow, as high clouds scudded hopefully, and destinies were sealed. Think of the terminal goodbyes too, still lingering on railway platforms – I sense them now – mingling with soot and steam (each young woman having bestowed a perfumed handkerchief on her love). Of the pledges given to the doomed militia men, as Isobel, May and Kathleen (known as Kitty) and Elsie and Anna and Chloe and sweet Lizzie Semple blew endearments, and of Phoebe who shamelessly kissed all the boys, superficially, at least, for luck. And of Hannah, Cissie, the smouldering Lily – of the valley – and her sister Dorothy who smoked, all bidding farewell. Consider every hanging kiss and trembling intimacy freely given before the guard blew his whistle, each whispered promise stashed in old kit bags, and of Arabella, with a certain look in her eye and her secrets.

How many fragile moons have waned since that gay parade of almost-flappers impressed light-sensitive paper, casting shadows on daylight but with no illumination of what would follow? Dark and umbral are the memories, if they exist at all, of who did what with whom – although I see them all.

No parents, of course. It was a party of sorts, and a wake – but who could tell the difference – a celebration and an echo of the tragic boys' departure. A rite of passage. And so many delicate hands in fashionable gloves, some climbing to the elbow.

Isobel had been with Ian, spooning and that, for ages. May kept company with Morris, unchaperoned, but he had a car. Kathleen had a crush on Kenneth, a keen horseman who rode to hounds. Elsie was walking out with Enright, poor thing, and Anna had been making eyes at Allan, spelled with two 'l's. Chloe preferred girls. No shame in that. She and Lizzie had smooched deliciously one amber twilight and felt on fire. Phoebe loved the sergeant to distraction, despite her innocent generosity to others. Hannah was mad about Henry. Just crazy. Cissie had become engaged to Charles, dear Charles with the charming turn in his eye, and Lily, who left her fragrance where ere she walked, simply adored her Laurance. All wonderful young women in their way.

Then there was Dorothy, who smoked.

Today and forever the house persists. I plod, at last, in a manner of speaking, its many potholed lane, riddled still with ruts and hidden slunks. The hills are littered deep yellow with nostalgic egg-yolk coloured whins. I scale the braes ethereally, for fear of stumbling even yet, in that wild rooty place, noting the many impromptu ponds which fail to drain. Of blighted livestock I see none, save two Irish hares who box, I expect, quite brutally. A linnet sings, her small heart fluttering, you understand. I broach the decaying dwelling, lingering spiritually on the very spot where everyone had gathered in a ghostly choir.

The grass still looks so bent.

Dorothy adored David to death, believe me. Her Adonis. And indeed, he was the most desirable of the young men by a damned long chalk. Breathing smoke kisses directly into his lungs, she had given herself to him. Entirely. Insanely. And had drunk much wine from his wicked goblet, more than bleeding once. She had been his thoroughly, she'd thought. And he would be hers when Johnny, as it were, came marching home. Hurrah.

In that ancient likeness, to the right of the delectable Arabella, dear child, the most engaging of the girls, by far – is there a parallel – many have perceived an extra shadow. An illusion perhaps? The picture has been studied by scholars. The spectral beckoning of some presence has been remarked. But no, I could not possibly say.

'Look, look, it's occult, like the Shroud of Turin,' someone insisted, but others laughed.

Who was her beau? That was the question, until person or persons discovered the rollicking truth. Tell it not in Gath. The rest is history, though not well known. Which of the young men in that troop of lolling heroes leaning fatally from the windows of the train, in the sulphurous farewell fumes of the diabolic black engine, had been enticed by the cunning Arabella?

In the picture, she stands next to Dorothy, whose cigarette burns perilously close to the porcelain skin of Arabella's arm.

Inside the house, these days, a thousand spiders weave webs, consuming their wingless prey at will. In a decaying window two hurricane lamps sit wickless, waiting for virgins. Ha, and where are they? Suspended on a bulging wall, a cracked mirror hangs akimbo. Besmirched art deco. I see a corroded radio, from some later period. A pale horse's fraying harness. A brittle noose of rope. In the inglenook a gin trap grins, retained by the current owner, a skinner who visits occasionally to, reputedly, eat young leverets. Deep in the damp recess of the pantry, a fluted bottle lurks. Green, poisonous fluid, no doubt. Half full. A metallic pot weeps oxide tears.

Dorothy was no fool, let me tell you. Each puff from her well-formed mouth contained an elegant dose of vitriol, justifiable I might add, and in the photograph, one may perceive in her, without much trouble, more than a trace of hatred, though prettily displayed through even teeth. I'll leave that to yourself.

At any rate, after the birthday tea, for such it was, and the extinguishing of eighteen of the slimmest candles, thoughtfully arranged by Phoebe, some person or persons, as I say, led Arabella blindfolded, in a manic romp, admittedly, to the cliff edge, where they left her in the dark, for reasons apparent to themselves. I'll let you guess. The corporeal embodiment of the shadow, perhaps, if it was real? She, foolish girl, had believed it to be some game of bluff, though it was quite a hike, and several times she stumbled pitifully.

'Is it much farther?' she asked in that duplicit little voice. She, who knew every blade, each vetch and waving trefoil.

'This will teach you,' laughed her guide or guides, in mock frivolity. 'Tell us of your lover, Arabella,' they said, prancing in little dainty shoes, 'and you shall be set free.' Arabella refused to speak.

How do I know all this? Don't ask. Who saw them leave for the high rockheads? No one appeared to know. Perhaps they flounced so wildly to the sawing fiddles that an evil magic possessed them or could they have become besotted by the languorous airs of the box player, a drunken foreign chap, who later could not be found? At any rate, I'm sure their bodies, at times, swayed fabulously with womanly poise. Or there again, had their heels clacked heedless and hell-bent in the lamplight? Were they heady and bewitched with brew? Wisely, they never said. I saw to that.

One hundred feet below the precipice, said the RIC, on the sea-crash shelf of crabs, she lay alone, her cries presumably ignored by cormorants, then sinking to the cruel ebb of gannets off the stacks. A desperate sight, trust me, it must have been.

I find the place easily enough. Shove in the reticent door of the junk room. Hear its rustic creak. Tread soft on fractured wormwood boards, feel them want to yield but, weightless, I creep among dismembered dolls and one-eyed bears and bins of mildewed books belonging, as they inform the reader on mottled flyleaves, to 'Arabella Woebegone' – not her real surname. The hand was lavish, as you may imagine, belonging to none other than herself. No doubt she'd grasped her own perfidy perfectly, even then.

Lighted only by the tiniest window, I find the hiding place, as I expect, brim full of dried-up lilac pens and purses, and under them in a recess, the single glove, wizened now, though supple leather once, and purchased in Brown Thomas on that memorable excursion to Dublin, when promises were made to me. Ah, do not speak of that. There it lies, white with mites and the dust of death. I could have fetched it years before, but the time seemed never right.

'Put them on,' I'd said to her before the high cliff walk. 'Go on, you know you want to.' She'd smiled her hidden smile.

Above my head, the pink paw scuttle such houses harbour. I lift the glove reverently, in reunion, and feel a forbidden thrill. I do it out of respect. Not for her, but for him. For David, who had bought them, lest it should fall apart. I do not blame him. Nor did I ever, for any man would have done the same. I knew what she was. The glove may fall apart, dredged as it is, from an age below. But Lord, it holds. It holds too well. Sweet God, inside, I find her fingers still. Tiny refined bones. Twisted, complex, tricky digits, delicate, slender and cropped off neatly, as I recall – by a stone-ground axe or cleaver, I should remember, and probably with one cut.

'Ah yes,' I say, blue with carcinogenic grace. 'That's right. One cut.'

Auf Wiedersehen

I think I knew she wasn't my real Aunt Lizzie. She wasn't even Dad's. I'd never met a woman like her. Nobody I knew had. For a start she had a man's voice. Not like one of those vulgar fog horns that sounded when mist came in. No, it was gravelly, like the crunch of walking on shingle, or a pulverising machine churning in a stone pit or a lorry's gearbox, before we had synchromesh. She quarried words like boulders deep in her gullet, and rolled them out like a fast bowler. Woe betide if she'd connected, but somehow, I knew that she liked me.

It must have been late in nineteen forty-two when I went to stay at Binford with Aunt Lizzie. We'd survived the blitz at home, but Dad had his sermons to write and, well, he wanted a bit of peace after all that had happened. He left me off in the leathery black Morris, with its tight little bucket seats.

'Did you bring your comb and jar of Brylcreem?' he asked. Old Dad was a stickler for partings.

Aunt Lizzie told me to carry my little bag of tricks, that's what she called it, to the attic, where I was to live. It was a sloping refrigerator up there, three storeys above the world. The bed was narrow, like a shelf. I lifted a Gideons' Bible that nobody had opened. I could tell by its spine and the smell of glue that it was new, and unloved.

By the time I trudged back down the stairs, Dad was gone. Well gone, like a vapour, as it says somewhere. That was him, always needing to get along. And that was it, till he came back for me. Not a scrap did I hear. I didn't hear from mother either, but then she'd been 'Taken', so that was different.

When the war ended, he was ever so glad to see me, he said, though, to be honest, I don't think he recognised me. Not really, and definitely not right away. Do you know, if he'd passed me by in Binford Main Street, peering through the window of the model train shop or the bakery, he might have raised his hat, like he did to women, and said, 'Good morning.'

'You've got to be a big lad, Ian,' was what all he said, like he was admiring a chrysanthemum, 'a right big lump.' He spoke like that for fun. Good old Dad. He thought it was amusing. 'I've come to take you home to meet your new mother,' he said. 'Now what do you think of that?'

I didn't speak.

'You're going to like her,' he said, 'she's a bobby dazzler.'

I didn't want a bobby dazzler.

But that was later.

'You'll have a sup of beef tea,' Aunt Lizzie growled. She was in the kitchen, stirring a delft mug. I recognised the aroma because I'd visited a farm near Chapham once, when I was five, and the lady gave us Bovril. I've been blessed with a good memory.

I didn't have to talk. It was all right to be quiet. So, I sat on her horse-hair sofa, though I recall it as unyielding. I thought they might have shaved the horses, lathering them up, you know, the way Dad did, with his little wobbling brush, and applied a cut throat razor, though it would have taken a while.

I don't know if you're familiar with horse hair. It's a prickly customer. All those little wiry strands that would give you a rash. I wore short trousers then. Grey tailored. You don't see them now. It's amazing, when

I think of it, how much skin there is on a boy's bare legs and how firm and tight it was then.

'Have a digestive biscuit,' Aunt Lizzie said, and I did, testing the tiny holes with the tip of my tongue. It was soft and grainy, with a bluish tinge of mould. Like penicillin, or something growing between your toes. I didn't remark on it. Dad had taught me manners.

'You're not like your dad,' Aunt Lizzie rasped, 'you're not like him at all.'

She was right. I favoured mother. I have her nose. She died on the railway. That's how she was 'Taken', suddenly, one Friday on the train. Just north of junction five. They reckoned the door was loose. She'd fallen out.

'Your mother jumped,' Aunt Lizzie said, just like that.

She took me unawares, coming out with it. I wasn't ready for it. I was only twelve, so I said, 'I beg your pardon,' and she said it again.

'Leapt to her death from a moving carriage. Hadn't a chance.'

Dad had never told me. I wondered if she'd jumped because of me.

'I'm exasperated with you, Ian,' she used to tell me, and I knew that she was. 'You're a dreamer, like your dad. And you're always scribbling.'

I know I liked to write. Stories, and the occasional poem. Nothing wonderful, but it was all I ever wanted to do, and it made me feel alive. I wondered if that was so bad?

'Come with me to Flo's,' she'd say. Flo was her friend. I didn't fancy her – I don't mean that the way it sounds. She was a middle-aged woman with whiskers, and a mole. It was more that… well, they never talked of anything. Just sat and said, 'Isn't this nice?' or 'Would you like more tea?' 'I recall Mother saying, 'Old Mr Quentin's took to his bed, poor soul.' Her grammar could be poor at times. Dad often corrected her. She and Flo were forever discussing souls.

'Now remember, Gertrude' – that's what he called her – '*I* go in the name of the Lord, but, Thou God seest *me*.' He'd tell her that to illustrate the different cases, but she never took it in. Subjects and objects were lost on her.

'I won't go back to Flo's,' I told her. I was still a child, but sometimes I thought she was as well.

'Will you become a Reverend gentleman, like your dad?' she asked me more than once. It was funny that, the way she put it. I never answered. I thought it was what was called 'rhetorical'.

Dad preached at her funeral. Without notes. 'Well why would I ask another man to do it?' he said. 'If I were a plumber and I had a burst, I'd fix it myself.' He didn't cry. 'Without are dogs,' was his text. Mother was 'Within,' I hoped.

My new mother was there, in waiting, though I didn't know it then. Well, not that day. She was wearing a wide-brimmed hat with waxed fruit on it. A Miss Tetley. Like the tea. I only knew her to see. I should have asked him about the dogs, but I didn't, and the moment passed.

After Mother, Dad's head was up the chimney for a week or two. That's what I thought. Right up. I didn't want to bother him. By gum though, he was a man for length, with his long sighs and rows of theology books. 'I'm not over keen on these short homilies, Son,' he said, 'we're not Roman Catholics. We go for scripture and verse.' He was good like that. Always ready with a word in season. Then he mentioned Aunt Lizzie. 'You'll love it up there with her,' he said, 'there'll be lots of air.'

I can't say that I liked the blackout much. Who did? Cars with slits for illumination, and powdered eggs. 'Hitler will be snooping tonight again,' Dad used to say, 'turn off your bedside light or he'll spy you.'

It was hard to believe, but I did what he said.

'Are you scared of Hitler?' Aunt Lizzie asked.

I was sure I ought to be.

'He's a pox,' she said, apparently without thinking. I'd never heard a word like 'pox'. Not used like that. Only the chicken pox. I imagined the Führer all covered in spots, like a leopard with his thin moustache.

'Oh dear,' I said.

'What does a city boy do?' she asked, lighting up.

Mother had never smoked.

'A boy must always do something,' she said.

'I like to write,' I said. I thought she might be sniffy, like Dad, but next morning, good enough – I remember it was pouring – she produced a velvet box, tied with a bow. It smelt fusty like the olden days.

'You can use that in the study,' she said. 'Put on your outdoor things or you'll atrophy.' I'm sure that was the word she used. 'And mind the ghosts.'

Dad didn't hold with ghosts.

I remember wearing a blue woolly hat that Mother had knitted, like a tea cosy without the hole for the spout, and a pair of mitts, with a double string that held them together. I wasn't sure I could write in mitts, but I held my tongue. Aunt Lizzie was right. You could have frozen, like Lot's poor wife, in there.

I liked the grand piano though. The long, curved lid, the low notes grumbling like a giant's stomach or water tumbling in a cave. I wished I'd learned to play, but I'd never bothered. So much of life is like that. Missed chances.

There were pictures of pheasants everywhere. Like they had all arrived together off the bus one day in spring, and they'd stayed for keeps. Two stuffed ones strutted on the hearth. Upright, but stiff and dead, if you know what I mean. I thought they would singe their feathers. But the fire was never lit. There were snaps of huntsmen, faded badly, and a bugle belonging to some warrior in the war.

'The Boer War,' Aunt Lizzie said, as I tried to blow it. 'Keep going,' she said, 'there must have been a knack. The boy who played that instrument lies dead, somewhere in Africa,' she said. 'Pinioned by a spear, no doubt.' I'd never heard of 'pinioned' but I wasn't keen on it.

'Maybe you'll try something less dangerous, like tennis,' she said, 'there is a girl who sometimes comes. I'll get you a pair of pumps.' She looked at my feet. 'Size six, I assume?'

I wasn't sure.

The writing box contained at least five quires of creamy stationery and some ancient dipping pens, pots of Quink, black and blue, and a pad of blotting paper. We used that then. A mottled green if I recall.

'You should sit at Great Grandpa's desk,' she said, 'his name is on the notepaper.'

It was. Embossed. 'Percival J. Mendips.'

'You've heard of him?'

I hadn't.

'It wasn't his real name,' she said. 'He adopted it.'

In the second week the girl came twice, a flaxen fairy out of nowhere.

'You must be the boy?' she said. 'Do you speak German?' She sang, and smelled of pines. 'What do you do?' she asked, just like Aunt Lizzie.

'I'm writing a novel,' I said. I hoped I would.

'That must be a bore,' she said, 'inventing plots and things, making good triumph over evils. I shouldn't like that at all. Do you like to play the hockey?'

An extra word can convey a lot.

'It looks too fast,' I said, 'scampering after the ball.' I thought I should be honest.

'All right,' she said, 'let's walk down to the maze.'

I'd never seen a maze.

'Oh yes,' she said, 'life is full of surprises.'

I asked her who she was.

'What has that to do with anything?' she said. 'Let's go and get confused.'

Sometimes she spoke in jerks. She asked if I was a sport. What could I say?

'Six hundred feet and forty twists,' she said, 'built out of British yews.'

I'd thought of hedges as living things.

'I'll lead you to the centre,' she said. 'Blindfolded you shall be, and then, when I clap my hands and shout, "Go", you will escape.'

I hoped I could.

She bound my eyes quite tightly. 'No peeping,' she said.

I was in there for some time. I don't know how long exactly. 'Keep going,' she called from somewhere. I didn't panic but I did not love the maze.

'I'll give you a prize,' she shouted, 'if you can exit without my help. I shall kiss you… on the lips. So there. Should you like that?'

'I've never been kissed,' I said, 'well, not since Mother died. And not on the lips.'

'Excellent,' she said.

'Do you enjoy playing with the girl?' Aunt Lizzie asked. 'She tells me she likes your style.'

What was my style?

The spirit of the Mendips Man – I named him that – lived in the parlour. His presence floated in the stuffy air like old tobacco smoke. I breathed it each time I sat in his swivel chair. I made it spin, and thought of ships and pirates. I don't know why.

'You should try it,' I told the girl.

But she wouldn't. 'Shall you read to me?' she asked.

'Do you not read?' I said.

'I read Russian, French and German. But I desire enchantment.'

'Why are you here?' I asked, but this was pointless.

'And you?' she said.

I believe I shrugged. Often she came on Thursdays and stayed till Monday.

'Shall you come with me to church?' she asked.

Aunt Lizzie was an atheist and swore profanely. 'Go if you like,' she said, flicking ash, 'as long as you know it's bunkum.'

The girl wore a straw boater with a ribbon. 'How rosebud English do I look, or don't you care?' she said. 'I'm set to sing a solo.'

The church was tiny and full of plaques to dead soldiers. Her voice was 'Mezzo,' she said, 'unusual, I'm told'. She must have been fourteen. The vicar gave her flowers.

One evening, after dinner, she took me to the summerhouse. The turquoise paint was peeling. It was a place of woodlice, of cricket bats, linseed oil, and mice, perhaps?

'I want to ask you something,' she said, standing so close I could feel her breath blow warmly on my face, 'shall you love me no matter what?'

Something stirred inside me. I know I smiled. She played piano well. Chopin, deliciously. After the kiss, I had begun to love her madly.

On a dull, wet, summer afternoon, we sat in that summerhouse on crocheted cushions. She taught me the rules of chess. 'The aim is to deceive,' she said. 'How versatile is my queen? You see, your king is quite surrounded?'.

As final bombs fell far away, we rambled through the willow, looking for wizards and wiccans. That sort of thing, for we were children. Aunt Lizzie had packed smoked salmon and there was ginger pop.

'Shall we take bicycles?' said the girl, one glorious day. We rode the dusty road to Binford, she and I, eyes streaming, like actors in a film. Her blond hair fairly flew. Too fast we rushed down lanes and by canals, stopping at smart stone bridges to admire the boats.

'Take us, please, for a ride,' she asked a bargee with a pipe.

'He'll do no such thing,' said his wife, brown skinned, and angry as a hornet. And do you know, in all that time, I never thought of Dad. Not once.

'Do you think I'm a good kisser?' she asked.

'I like kissing,' I said. And it was true. I did. I liked her kissing me.

'Also, you can do some other things,' she said, but she never told me what. I didn't ask. I didn't know a lot.

'Shall you miss me?' she asked.

'Are you going away?' I said hoarsely.

The war was almost over.

Aunt Lizzie listened to the wireless. A loud, vibrating box affair. 'Oh yes,' she said, inhaling deeply, 'old one-ball Hitler's had his chips.'

I thought it a strange thing for an elderly lady to say, but I held my tongue.

'Will you write for me a poem?' said the girl. 'Before I go?'

I had no idea where she was going, but I said I would. It was about swallows migrating, and spawning fish, swarming bees, bindwood and Robin Run the Hedge. I wasn't sure that she'd like it, but I gave it to her anyway, the day she left.

I don't remember all of it now, but the last line was something like, 'And so my life is ending just as I begin.' It was an awkward way to put it and I hoped she'd understand. 'Begin' may have rhymed with chin. Her chin. She had a dimple in the middle.

After I read it to her, she replaced the poem in its smooth envelope, like something precious and I was shocked when she began to sob. I reached for the linen handkerchief I carried then. Aunt Lizzie boiled them in a special pot.

I'd written the poem in blue, because I thought it would be best. I suppose it must have got to her. I wrote, 'To the Girl with the Golden Locks'. I still didn't know her name. She hadn't said. I had been glad when the ink flowed on smoothly. The blotting paper had that dry feel you never get these days.

'For me?' she'd asked in her grown-up voice.

It was for her.

She left one Sunday in a grand Mercedes Benz, just as peace was declared. Bleakly, I watched her wave.

'So, what did you think of our Ingrid?' Aunt Lizzie said, lighting another cigarette.

'Ingrid. Is that her name?' I whispered. 'I'll love her till I die.' I was surprised at what I'd said.

Aunt Lizzie nodded. Dad had always despised emotion.

'Her English is impeccable, don't you think?' she said, blowing several blue rings of smoke.

'It is,' I said. But I felt puzzled.

I imagine I was too young to understand. But I knew she was referring to something beyond me. Something big. It was a perplexing time, the war.

I mostly thought of Ingrid when I went to bed alone, when I lay cold as a corpse, without a hot water bottle, between the stiff white sheets, back home with Dad and my new mother, the bobby dazzler. You don't forget a girl like that.

I wondered for a long time if she ever thought of me. I suppose I still do.

Derry Red

Let me tell you the truth. Russia was the real winner of World War Two. Her subsequent cultural theft campaign would make the Nazis look like rag-and-bone men, believe me. Here's a for instance.

Gorsky, aka John Williams, was alone in Derry on the night before Christmas – the first since the guns went silent. Even by Russian standards the frost was cruel. Holly twigs snapped. Limbs ached. Snatched kisses hung numb under mistletoe. The air crackled. Ominously, the hands of the Guildhall clock had seized.

From his vantage point on the walls, he looked down on a deserted Guildhall Square. The sad yule spruce. The crib in the corner. Baby Jesus, blue-lipped no doubt and starving. No Magi. Only a hobbled ass lay chomping hay with his rough old tongue. 'Hee-haw,' he brayed across the Foyle. Sorrow skittered up King Street on the Waterside. The last, rickety train had long since chugged east on thin, razor rails. It was a night of contracting fishplates, of bolts shearing, but Gorsky was full of expectation.

Turning his key to the Britannia Hall, he climbed the squat, stone tower, smiling illicitly. An honorary Medal of Glory would soon be his. In the shadows, he poured from a dented Thermos and toasted the nativity, not with coffee, but with vodka, and without a belief in God. The city of song was silent. No crying was made by this unbreached maiden. Not yet. But she would be taken easily. In the recesses of his greatcoat, he stroked the gun metal of his TT 33. To his left, unseen, arose the Catholic pinnacle of St Eugene's. On his other side behind him, the planter cathedral gloomed, dense with relics of the siege. Both housed their share of darkness. Stars beamed false consciousness.

In overcrowded cots, the proletariat slept. Within the mansions of Victoria Park, the bourgeoisie slumbered, full of Cognac. The Americans had mostly gone. German U-boats lay scattered on the seabed, scuttled and murky. Good luck to them. The Brits had lost their air force. So much for Spitfires. History was on his side. Millions had given their lives for the motherland but there was more to do. Unfinished business for Stalin, whose boorish reputation was a bogus western myth.

Lights twinkled in Rosemount and over Brandywell, in a kind of

tranquillity blanket. Rationing would not end for a while. In the heavens, the Great Bear yawned and stretched his limbs. In the morning, children would awake to meagre, utility offerings with gratitude, but there would be more to think of.

The river, in its wisdom, had coagulated plenteously. Ice backing on ice, cracking and straining with prescience, could hardly contain itself. Overlooking the Bogside, the stony-faced Walker pointed a Protestant finger. The Lord would break the boom. Walker could not have foreseen what Gorsky knew.

Gorsky had been gifted in languages, and had won a scholarship to London in the thirties. Seen Mosley and his Blackshirts breaking heads. In Greek Street he'd read Marx and caught the vision, taken to Cyrillic script like a Muscovite and joined the Party.

He pictured the vast vessels, anchored at Lisahally, droning deep down, shafts thumping their beat. In his groin, he witnessed an erotic throb. In his head, the grind of gears. Oh, the sweet nectar of heavy oil, the fume clouds of the unloading monster ships with encrusted keels, settling in their berths, slick-decked, rime-hawsered after the run from Murmansk. From their cavernous bellies, armoured tanks would sweep into the city. And all thanks to his intelligence. Thanks to the street maps he'd named in Russian, the widths and gradients of roads that he had annotated; the camber and dimensions of every rutted lane noted, the gradient of Shipquay Street, the bearing loads of Craigavon Bridge. He had furnished it all in excellent time, to the last millimeter, and in coded letters, to the wily Novotnikov.

Sated dialectically with thoughts of Santa Claus, the simple people languished – open-mouthed, big-hearted, and coughing sporadically in their dreams.

Gorsky shone a narrow beam on his Vostok Amphibia. He noted the time: 2:20 am exactly. This was an eerie in-between hour, but it was well positioned. The Russians had docked. He'd seen their orange flare. Now he leaned over the city, on the parapet, savouring the moment, allowing himself to light a Sobranie, his one luxury. Thoughtfully, he watched it glow, inhaling an aromatic future, for once thinking warmly about himself.

The phoney festivities would unravel like his grandmother's old cardigan. She'd thought she caught it on a nail. Not so. At the age of ten, he'd mutilated the crafted wool and tugged it just enough. The fabric unspooled wondrously, in tight, grey maudlin curls, never to be reknitted. He'd maimed her kitten when he was bored.

After Hitler marched east, Gorsky, aka John Williams, had come to Derry to play his part. It was then he sought a welcome within the Boys. 'Why not?' they thought. He lent them a certain gravitas – oblivious as they were to the hammer and sickle tattooed on his buttocks by the delicious Kalenensky, after beer and borscht. An unusual treat for him, but very good, and bursting with flavour, like her, that once, in Little Russia, Tottenham.

Tonight, he had circled the walls like a nobody. But that would pass. Let Christmas creep miserably into Derry. He didn't care, for the Russians were coming in cavalcade, led by General Pushkin. Gorsky smoked and strolled to Dacre Terrace, to capture a first glance of their magnificence. There he would catch the first glimmer of dawn.

The tenth army rumbled on caterpillar tracks across the upper deck of the bridge, past the red brick fortress of Tilly's on their left (referenced in *Das Kapital*) and the clean-cut elegance of the Box Factory. The bridge held, as he had known it would. By now the city had stirred. Women in crocheted shawls gathered, agog in Wapping Lane, to gape at the fur-clad Soviets, who raised their hands, waving to a tiny group of Salvationists, struggling with a tuba. Sad creatures. The temperature was minus ten. Behind the tanks came lorries. They parked around The Diamond.

Girls from Bishop Street came, tripping in shawls, with steaming mugs of tea to warm the Russians. Reporters for the *Journal*, shivered and took snaps. The RUC arrived sleepily, for once, in an obsolete Crossley tender, but refused to draw their truncheons. Phone calls were made. The B Specials did not feature. The baffled sergeant had no Russian. There were too many to arrest, he assured his nervous constables.

The Mayor appeared in his chain, with several aldermen. 'Who was the head bombardier?' he wanted to know. There were shouts of 'Da,' and 'Net,' – as the soldiers took the walls. The Soviets had brought their own bulldozers and muscular squaddies with spades and picks. They consulted Gorsky's excellent scale drawings, measuring up and chalking out, like tailors, discrete great chunks of wall.

A mathematician flicked rows of balls on an abacus and barked instructions. Reinforced generators bumped into life. Deafening pneumatic drills were dragged unto the parapets, where a dreadful pounding began. The lorries waited. Someone mentioned the London Companies and King James the First. The Russians scoffed, breath streaming. Both bishops appeared, wearing tweed coats over pyjamas. The governor of the Apprentice Boys requested prayer. But who should pray first? Gorsky was at the docks.

A thousand metal barges had been tied up at the wharves, at McCorkell's Mills. They sparkled in the frost. Lighter men shouted. Gulls whirled.

Gorsky fingered his pistol, without expecting to use it. The unmistakable sound of rending rocks came from the Double Bastion, as ancient stones were ripped.

Logistics were his forte. The first of the laden trucks, each displaying a large red number, as he had suggested, descended the hill in low gear, passing banks and cafés, bulging with their blessed cargo.

For the duration of the day and in the weeks that followed, the sacred walls were demolished – wisely without interference by the authorities – in an orderly fashion and carted to the river to be loaded. From there, they were floated, in great flotillas to Lisahally, where the Soviet sailors winched the treasure into the holds of the *St Petersburg*, the gargantuan *Dnieper* and other craft, too numerous to mention. Gorsky did not intrude on Pushkin. He simply waited for instruction.

Opinion in the city was naturally divided. Nationalists had never loved the walls. Why would they? For the Apprentice Boys, though, their agony was complete. They wept as their heritage was looted. Gorsky kept out of sight, awaiting his moment, skulking among the brothels and pork butchers of Foyle Street. His time would come. The British, laughably, flew a snickering biplane above the site, taking aerial photos for the record, while de Valera ranted on Radió Éireann. He spoke in Irish, so few could understand him. Stormont issued limp condemnations, promising consequences. That raised a smile on many faces. Some urgent females got brawny Soviet men.

On the 1 April, ahead of schedule, the last shovelful of earth was extracted, the final capstone dismantled. Records were signed in triplicate. The walls were to be re-erected exactly in Red Square. This it appeared, had been a secret and longstanding ambition of the Russian leader. They took the cannon too, raising two fingers to The Honourable, The Irish Society, the Haberdashers, the Skinners, Goldsmiths and the rest.

The final, wheezing truck bore off old Roaring Meg, on which they'd hung a sign in English, saying, 'This gun belongs to Uncle Joe'. Some people cheered. Not many. The only thing left of any consequence was Walker on his pillar. It was said that the Russian robbers smirked, for they had a sense of humour.

As spring arrived, soft and willowy bees had ventured forth. By now, Gorsky had a full beard and had been sleeping in a disused house in Mountjoy Street. This was a game he understood. Anonymity for the cause. The Russians would keep him protected until the last moment. Then they would pipe him aboard. There would be Cossack dancing and huzzas.

As a professional, he played along, quietly tracing where the walls had stood since 1618. Five years to build; three months to remove. Now only a lime scab surrounded the plantation city. People picked their way around it like crows, saying, 'Sweet Mother,' and, 'Oh my glory,' depending on their preference. Catholics and Protestants mingled in a muddled sort of way.

The Soviet fleet had built up steam, and groaned to be off. To bear the walls away. Gorsky set off in good time to join them on his stolen Rudge bicycle, to take his passage, to receive his just deserts; a handsome pot of roubles, and a new life, twenty-five kilometres from Leningrad.

But the giant anchors had been weighed. The gangplanks pulled. The Russians had got what they came for. All of it. To the last pebble. They did not need him now, and had left without him. On a rising tide they were already half a mile from the shore, and piling on knots. Plumes streamed from the implacable steel smokestacks of the people's navy. The mocking blasts from the communist ships' horns were only deafening.

Like a shorn lamb, Gorsky, aka John Williams watched the fleet grow smaller. With empty eyes, he followed their disappearing, grey silhouettes. Surveying their filthy wake, he studied the bobbing flotsam, the eddying wreathes of foetid foam, and finally pondered his life. What had it been? With sudden ferocity, a robin chittered on a leafless alder, protecting its territory, little bastard that it was.

At last, the sea swallowed the ships and with them, the walls. Stripped of everything, Gorsky fumbled for his 33, grasping it like the proffered hand of a perfidious friend.

Closing the Lid

Libby lost her mother in March. In September, her reclusive second cousin Lydia visited, against the diktat of her sect. She was undoubtedly a pallid, haunted woman, oddly swaddled like a nun before her time, with downcast face, and self-reproachful eyes. Her hair, always dark and abundant, had been grabbed cruelly by a clasp with teeth, and trapped. She wore it like a crown of thorns.

'I felt, after all, that I ought to call,' she said in distant nasal tones. Perhaps she was a pilgrim, like Jesus, but more alone.

Libby had fussed and baked a salmon, set out the floral china. She had curled up pats of butter. For garnish, there was a sprig of parsley. The unusual centrepiece of bronze chrysanthemums was entirely for her guest. 'Anna, here, will take your hat,' she said, prompting her daughter, in a soft, grey voice. 'Did you know, pet,' she said to Anna, 'that Lydia and I once gathered bluebells like twins together, in the spring?'

Anna, who was ten, and still believed in fairies, found this hard to imagine, but she stretched out a willing hand, the way young people did, and smiled, 'I can take your hat,' she said.

Lydia pressed her beret to her head. 'Thank you, no,' she told the child. 'I'll keep it on. You know that I may not eat with you,' she said to Libby, who somehow, had thought an exception might be made, that

Lydia – out of compassion, and because they had once been close as girls – might have bent the rules. But no. She saw that now. There would no breaking of bread together. Lydia's light had been extinguished. Her regime took precedence.

Accordingly, she installed her without a careless word in their tiny sitting room, in the company of the upright piano and pink-paraffin heater. In the sanctuary of her kitchen, though, she shook her head, and wept for the sheer crookedness of it, as she arranged, with grace, a solitary tray. Sadness may have lurked behind the round lenses of Lydia's spectacles, but if Lydia had ever considered escape, as surely she must, that time had come and gone.

Lydia's father James, had wrenched himself free of his roots fifty years before, fleeing the cold blasts of north Antrim, and travelling light, with a small inheritance and plenty of ambition. Stepping from the hissing train, in snow, he had landed in a tram-clang city of rivets and bottled porter, red hot with ungodliness, and hardened by shipyard men.

He sought the merchant classes; dreamed of owning a grocery emporium and to that end, married Christa, one of the Hemphills, an affluent freethinker, if not a rank agnostic. In this, he supposed he had grieved the Lord, but the earthly gain was great. He might have joined an Orange Lodge, but chose instead an assembly of the Closed Believers – a mournful, industrious sect, who, after checking his credentials, advanced him a loan at four per cent. He secured a red brick dwelling in Stranmillis to house his aspirations.

By the age of forty, and far from the peat reek of his origin, James, who had paid back the loan, had also abandoned the glottal stop and was buying his shirts in Arthur Street. The sun shone on his success, as he lorded it over his own ample counters. His apprentice, Sloan, was a dapper young gallant with strong legs and ambition. James Murray's Delicatessen was the talk of the town for sides of ham and Portavogie prawns.

Lydia, born in 1920, was moulded by her father and not by Christa, her cerebral mother, who lacked maternal instinct. Lois came next: 'Another immaculate conception,' some people said. She loved to sing for joy. But the Closed Believers deplored that sort of thing. As for Christa, she demanded silence in the home, where she mounted dead moths, with pins, upon the walls.

Each Sunday morning, at the stroke of nine, James read the Bible bleakly, to the girls. By then Christa had left to meet her worldly chums, a godless squad of ramblers, several of whom rode bicycles and were lepidopterists. Seldom did she return until the evening.

Lois may have shimmered with potential in her soul, but her body shrivelled in the shoebox halls in which the Believers met. One day her sagging spirit fled to join the angels.

Something must have died in Lydia too, without an occupation or a man. For a period, after the war, she sought employment as a lady's companion, but so very much had changed. She considered teaching privately. It was not to be. When, after one soaking too many, Christa also trod the valley of the shadow, James required Lydia to reign at home. An empty queen lacking purpose, at almost thirty.

On occasion, it was true, she had helped him in the shop, but as a man of substance now, he did not encourage it. She had also cared, at times, for a neighbour's invalid daughter, but her work was undervalued and short-lived.

As summers shrank, time whirred her life away. Like some Victorian ward, she practised embroidery and painting in the chilly attic, using only the palest washes. Naturally, James refused to hear of her cooking. Had he not hired Kathleen, from the Markets, for that activity?

At Easter, when the gorse was sprung, on the day of Lydia's birthday – always overlooked – two visiting preachers came to address what the Believers called their 'Conference'. The topic was 'Love'. She may have blushed at that. These good, lay brethren had journeyed from Seskinore, to lodge with her and James.

Kathleen opened their windows and aired their double bed – sharing was a common practice then – providing them with towels and jugs of steaming water, for travelling made one grubby.

The older was Cleghorn, a widower, who spoke with pathos of the Cross – what greater love? – dwelling on the blood of Christ. He also explained in detail, some rampant errors creeping in. 'Be on your guard,' he said.

The other was a younger, single man, a bricklayer, it seemed, by day, whose name was Caldwell – perhaps a probationer disciple on trial. His workman's hands were hacked, but he knew the scriptures, and even joked a little, though his eyes, she thought, were troubled. It would be strange to hear his booming voice in the gloom of the dining room.

Lydia had heard a thousand sermons. Most of them interminable. But Caldwell's, that Easter morning, seemed altogether different.

'Do we want darkness in our hearts?' he said, smiling a brittle radiance. 'Why should we wait until we get to Glory to reflect His light? Love must excite and extend inside and out, above and beyond, and include, yes, I'll say it now, without a bit of shame, the... more intimate moments of privacy.'

Sweet Lord, what was this?

The Believers shuffled. Old Cleghorn coughed.

'Provided,' said Caldwell, 'our intentions are pure, let us surrender all our urges to His plans, and secure our own resurrection, in every sense, as well as remembering His. For, although we have been raised to life, we remain human, with honest human needs.'

Humanism was sin.

Lydia may have detected a rustling among the women, entombed as they were, within their bonnets. Christ had risen, it was true, but there was little reason for overt display. And to associate His triumph with... well what?... was out of place. She noted some lowering of feminine heads, rebelling at his words, for joy – if it came at all, was a tense and muffled affair. And God knows, lust was everywhere.

Did she imagine the eerie silence after that morning meeting, in James's capacious Bentley, as the transfigured apprentice Sloan – now wearing a smart, brushed, chauffeur's cap – wafted them back to Stranmillis for Kathleen's leg of lamb?

After a lengthy blessing, during which Cleghorn asked God to hallow the food, James carved the paschal flesh, slicing fiercely with his late wife's bone-handled knife. Lydia served each man in silence, leaning over their shoulders to pour rich gravy.

'More, if you please,' said Caldwell, neglecting the mint sauce, 'and is there any mustard?'

It was, she thought, a little forward, and out of place, poor man.

Without speaking, James dissected every morsel into regular fragments, stabbing with his fork at cubes of carrot, chewing the lamb slowly on account of his dentures and inoperable hiatus hernia.

After a creamy bread pudding, Cleghorn – who did not care for raisins – felt the want of air and suggested a river stroll. 'Show me something of God's floral carpet, James,' he asked obliquely.

Perhaps the preacher wished to speak to James alone.

'What about our friend?' her father said, squinting at Caldwell, and then at Lydia.

'I have some loose ends to check before this evening's meeting,' said Caldwell, reaching for his Bible.

Cleghorn sneezed.

'Put on your overcoat, Father,' said Lydia, 'for fear of the wind, and take a stick.' She accompanied them to the door.

'We must look to heaven for inspiration,' said James, staring at the sky. 'We'll not be long.'

Lydia and Caldwell sat in silence in the parlour, on opposite sides of the cold hearth, each well-defended by convention, staring at the empty grate, each thinking presumably, their own thoughts, inhaling the odour of encrusted soot. She studied the familiar Wilton carpet. The intricacies of its geometrical design, low heels digging into its woollen pile. He breathed in deeply through his nose. Though not unpleasantly. She inspected his sledgehammer hands, and then her own, noticing for the first time a raised little vein.

'I am looking forward to your gospel message this evening,' she told him, with some genuine anticipation.

Caldwell had strong squat fingers. 'What do you think of love and joy?' he asked directly.

'I have heard of them, of course,' she said. An attempt at humour. Perhaps she sounded coy.

'Ah, yes,' he said, 'but do you believe in what I was saying?'

'I believe that you know best,' she said, 'being a preacher and a man.' She did not mean to tease, exactly.

'Tonight, I will speak on, "Liberation".'

'The Good News brings us freedom from our sins,' she trotted out, listening to her voice as one might to a machine.

'Ah, sin is one thing,' said Caldwell, 'but I am speaking of the shackles... the manacles that...'

'Oh yes,' she said, too quickly, 'the grosser iniquities.' Whatever they might be.

'The rules of bondage,' he said.

Perhaps he would like some tea?

'For instance,' he said, 'I do not believe it can be loving to prevent an unsaved man from carrying the coffin of a friend. To refuse to let him take the departed to his final resting place. That can hardly be a human act.'

'But he would have to be the Lord's,' she said – the words came easily enough – 'before he could lift a Believer. Otherwise – well...' Her voice trailed off.

'That happened with my brother, you know,' said Caldwell. She did not know. 'He toppled from a roof.'

'That's sad,' she said.

'Yes, and they wouldn't let his pal convey him, for the committal at the grave. "Stand aside," they said, like Roman soldiers. Can you take that in? Could that be right? Where was the compassion?'

She could not say.

'You see,' said Caldwell, lifting the poker for something to hold, 'the Closed Believers are full of man-made rules, artificial calibrations that measure God's mercy like a standing length of timber. But there has to be more to it, surely. For God so loved the world.'

Her father would not be long. 'I hope they have remained upright,' she said, 'the gentlemen, I mean, though perhaps I see your point.' Why did she toy with him?

'Only perhaps?'

How dry her mouth had become. She was not being fair. 'There are so many lateral tree roots on the paths,' she said, 'I trust they have not tripped.'

'Or the sharing of food with unbelievers,' said Caldwell, who now could not be stopped. Another barbarity. He appeared quite rattled. 'I work on ordinary building sites,' he said, 'in mud, you know, and glar, where fellows mix plaster and stir cement and swear and curse, but we look out for each other, like mates. I understand all that. We sit down together for a sandwich and a drop of scald from flasks.'

'I'm sure you do,' she said. She'd heard these expressions in the shop, if not at her all-girls college.

'Let me tell you something then,' said Caldwell, brimming now with energy, 'the leaders of our Assembly want me to cut myself off for the whole lunchbreak. To actually position myself completely on my own, and chew my bit of bread, like a hermit. To have nothing at all to do with these boys that Christ Himself died for nearly two thousand years ago – to snub the precious souls that lay the bricks with me, hand over hand, day in and out, and treat them as... unclean.'

Like lepers, she almost said. She did feel the iniquity. She could not deny it.

'And will you comply?' she asked, 'or will you spurn the men appointed by the Lord?' Her lip no doubt had quivered.

'Look,' Caldwell said, 'maybe you already know this, but I'm here on trial as a preacher. All I want to do, is to reach people, for Jesus, to really speak to hearts. But sometimes, well, I just don't know. I put it to myself, sure what did He do, Himself?'

'He healed the sick,' she said, smartly, 'but I'm sure He never laid a brick.' She had said it with arrogance and bitterness, and out of anger. 'Oh glory,' she said. 'I do not mean to mock.'

But now this Mr Caldwell grinned, as though he had watched her slither on black ice. His eyes were brown and burnished – like handsome buttons wanting to be popped. He laughed in such an infectious way, it did her good and so she also laughed, albeit with less abandon. There should be mirth in joy, she dared to think.

If this seemed some relief, it was not to last, for her father, returning with Cleghorn, surveyed them in silence. Two ancient men, with mud spats on their shoes, regarding two younger humans in a heavy manner. They did not smile.

'What is all this merriment?' her father asked.

She wiped her eyes, one hand conflicted at her throat.

'Did you check your texts?' he said to Caldwell, roughly.

Oh mercy, what now?

Then Caldwell did an unlikely thing. He lied. Quite blatantly. 'Oh yes,' he said, 'I did indeed, with the help of Miss Murray here.'

She felt a thrill. In that moment it seemed as though he had lifted a lid, as if she had caught the whiff of something sweet, something truthful, free and forbidden, or that the Saviour Himself had extended His wounded hands to hers, like He did to Mary in the Garden.

But had she reached for His?

For his evening address Mr Caldwell wore a desperate yellow tie, and a bloom plucked from the garden. The dour Believers' Hall was thronged with saints. He delivered his thoughts awkwardly, in the end, she thought. He spoke of Mary Magdalene and how she had failed to recognise the Master. But when Jesus said her name, Mary's heart had melted. Her woman's pure passion had been aroused. Lydia scrutinised Caldwell's face, then glanced away. Some Brother said, 'Hallelujah,' and 'Yes Lord.'

Looking back, she would agree, it was ambiguous. Doubtless, Caldwell intended nothing personal, but he had embraced her directly with his gaze when he said the words. She found all this a trial.

'And are we so battened down,' he said – another reference to construction – 'that our joy has actually died? That it's still in the grave, bound head and foot, like the crucified One? Think about it, friends, on this resurrection day.'

She was thinking of little else. But what to do? What not to?

At first, she could not be certain, but now it seemed some signal had been exchanged between her father and the older preacher, who belatedly chose not to deliver his thoughts, but let things be, closing the gathering instead with a meandering prayer for guidance. Had Caldwell passed the test? Hardly. Had she? In his prayer, Cleghorn referred to some 'Crossroads,' before pronouncing the benediction. 'May grace mercy and peace… Amen.'

During that hour she had trawled her soul, seeking a basket to hold her thoughts, for a word that might define them. But when she found it, it was neither 'love' nor 'joy', but 'void'. Yes, that was it. An ugly, hollow vastness. The antithesis of life. It was a night of collision.

Then Sloan arrived, all business, to whisk the men away. To drive them to the bus. They thanked her disjointedly outside the hall, Caldwell allowing his ungloved hand to envelop her own, for a whisper longer than was required. She avoided his eyes. The die had been cast. It would become her way.

'May the Lord bless you and keep you as the years go by,' he said – he was not to know it was her birthday – 'and bring us together again if He sees fit.' She had not been mistaken. Cleghorn fidgeted. Her father consulted his watch. 'Ah well,' said Caldwell, 'you never know.'

But the challenge had been too great. In truth, she knew exactly, without any need to ponder the regular puffs of smoke from the Bentley's exhaust, the collateral drops of vapour falling, that the clouds had parted, oh so briefly, only to close again.

James asked a Brother to take them home. He suddenly looked older. More worn and in need of care. His grocer's brow had fallen, like an instep. The house would remain a tomb.

Rain threatened.

'Were there many bluebells, Father?' she asked. It seemed a century since she had picked wild flowers with Libby.

'What's that?' he said.

'When you walked, with Mr Cleghorn?'

'Ah Cleghorn,' he murmured. 'The bluebells were ruined. Some boys had romped in them with dogs. They were bruised and spoiled.'

Did he even remember Libby, when Lois and she had played with her and dreamed of princes? When gloom met gaity.

Then it came in a rush. 'Pray for Cleghorn, will you?' her father said – his voice was harsh. 'That fellow Caldwell's not worth a ball of blue – some preacher he would make. I told Cleghorn to turn him down. May God deliver us. I'm sure you see that too.'

'I understand,' she said, gripping his arm. But climbing into the Brother's sad Austin, she heard a shutter slam shut inside her head. The grind of metal. Steel screwed to steel.

'I'm sure you're right, Father,' she would tell him, her eyes filling on the threshold of the dead house, as she turned her key once more in the reluctant lock, her flat, dull, lingering key. Braced alone, before the mirror in the hallway, she snatched finally at her dark reflection. God knew her heart. So why had she not grasped the simple truth, held it up, steadied it like a full cup and drunk deep? She did not know, she told herself, why she had let it slip.

But this was self-deception, for, after all, it had been an act of will. A deliberate sin of omission, and by that sin, whatever its origin, she had crucified herself. She would, after all, become as one of her mother's tired moths. Those lifeless, dusty, former creatures, circumscribed, airless behind glass, and slowly fading over time. She knew then, that she would pay the price.

Forever.

Cave Painting

The Morning

Dawn stole across an ancient sea.

'I'm in love,' said Grinder, throwing back his yak skins, shivering in the coastal dankness of the cave, confiding to his friend, Gimlet.

'Is it the same woman?' growled Gimlet, who was cave cleansing.

'No, it's the Lady of the Sky,' said Grinder, who was hooked and who liked to be mysterious.

'What's her real name?' Gimlet asked, sweeping out two weeks' debris.

'The Moon,' said Grinder. 'Aim high, that's what I say.' He picked his incisors with a twig. 'And she loves me.'

'I've never seen you with her,' said Gimlet, who was a good sleeper and who had heard this sort of thing before.

'She plays hard to get,' said Grinder, who was a little bushed. 'Is there anything to eat? I adore watching her.'

'I'm sure she doesn't love being stared at all night by you, and would you ever lift your feet?' said Gimlet, hitting him a slap with the besom. 'I wouldn't want you staring at me. You can have what's left of those bison ribs.'

'I'm fed up looking at bison,' said Grinder, peering into a leather bucket. 'Did you mix the paint? We're low on ochre. You'll need to burn some charcoal. And melt down tallow. This cave is one dark hole. And it's freezing.'

'Lack of sleep,' said Gimlet. 'Early man collect no wood, he get no fire. Without fire, early man perish.'

'Yeah, but I'm dying for a boiled auk's egg,' said Grinder, who enjoyed his breakfast.

'You ate the last one yesterday,' said Gimlet. 'What is this lady like?'

'She's totally lunar,' said Grinder, splashing a very little cold water under his arms. 'All cloudy film and stuff. She wears a lot of white. But I like her in orange and I love her in red, though she never looks the same two nights in a row.'

'I'd like to meet her some time,' said Gimlet.

'Yeah, well, let's see,' said Grinder.

'You can trust me,' said Gimlet. 'I'm not going to run away with my friend's lover, now am I?'

'There's no chance of that,' said Grinder, stretching to his six foot nine.

'Why don't you invite her over some night to see the paintings,' said Gimlet, 'I'm sure she has great taste.'

'Too right,' said Grinder, examining his tongue. 'The Moon and me have a beautiful relationship. If she does come round, you'll see that for yourself. She only has eyes for me.'

Painting

The early men were painting cave horses, one each, in rusty laterite reds and yellows and blacks, using moss and lichen to sponge on colour.

'This rock's not great for holding the tinctures,' said Grinder, 'but at least you can see my horse. Yours is all watery. It doesn't look like an actual wall painted gee-gee, that a lady would come to see. It's far too gentle. It's a wimp. Mine's a beast. Your horse is too thin. I'm painting a fleshy animal for my queen. She'll be ecstatic. What do you say?'

'I keep telling you,' said Gimlet, short-handled brush between his jaws, 'I can't talk when I'm working.'

'But just look at my horse,' said Grinder. 'He's a pure savage. Gaze into his wild eyes. He's going to crack her up. Let's see yours again. No. I mean, what is it saying to the viewer? Softness, that's what. The Moon is a seasoned planet of the world.' Grinder sighed. He needed a break. 'And by the way, your horse's tail is much too long.'

The Afternoon

'I haven't seen her for a while,' admitted Grinder – who would leave all the brush rinsing to Gimlet. 'It's been too overcast. I've only caught tiny glimpses of her body.' He rubbed his giant paws together. 'But we're due some heavy nights. Wait till she sees me in my new winter fur. Were there ever two such heavenly bodies so intimately joined?'

'I'm sure,' said Gimlet, precision-shading his horse's belly with the feather of a goose.

'I'm thirsty,' said Grinder. 'Are you going to the well? She's so exciting. Sometimes, she's really slim, but then she fills out and glows, like a gorgeous fecund ball.'

'Uh-huh,' said Gimlet.

The Night

That night the Moon was full. But she was hidden. Grinder looked up, and roared his caveman's roar. The bats in the cave trembled. He could bay more loudly than Gimlet. Easily. And for longer. Grinder was a true savage, hair slick, backcombed and deadly. With a crimson bow of entrails about his neck, he flashed his fangs, terrifying the cave spiders.

'What time are you expecting her?' asked Gimlet, who was washing up.

'At ten,' said Grinder, chewing his claws, 'don't get upset if she's taken up with me. She won't mean you any harm. But she's a man's Moon, if you know what I mean, and she'll want to see my steed, how big and strong he is. I've brewed up burdock roots and made a beer. Hang around for a while, if you like.'

Gimlet was raking up ends of haematite, clearing the cave of rodents, though they were hard to shift. Trimming rush wicks.

Grinder fussed, parading in and out of the cave, fretting, squatting on the uneven floor, gazing into a wooden bowl of spring water at his reflection, squeezing pimples, scraping his face with a freshly sharpened flint.

Gimlet meditated, dwelling on the magnitude of the universe, repeating his mantra, 'Glide on,' which he found to be frictionless and calm inducing.

The Sky

The sky remained black until their donkey brayed ten times. Now Grinder was on his feet, out on the scree, stumbling, and staring at the heavens. Looking out to sea. Where was she? Not even a star peeped. 'Tonight's my night,' he told himself. 'She'll sleep with me – after she's seen my horse.'

Like a true Spirit she was late. Then, without warning, the firmament cracked, and there in voluptuous splendour shone the Moon in gossamer, twice as bright as Grinder had ever seen her, reflecting off the ocean, moving through the air, skirts swishing, sailing diaphanous with the ease of a dolphin.

'I told you she would make it,' he said, shaking with passion.

The Moon said nothing but she beamed across the world into the cave through an arch in the wall. Silverfish scuttled. The bats shielded blind eyes and squeaked. The rats crept silently into cracks, nudging one another, like wise old men with whiskers. Gimlet sat shadowy, on a ledge.

Grinder looked around for his mate. He would be in the way, of course, like a big hairy gooseberry, but where had he gone? Grinder needed to be alone with the Moon. His loins ached for her. He could see that she wanted him. He poured her a frothy beer. She let it sit. She would sip it later. He fluffed up his bear suit. Several times. But she did not seem impressed.

At length he said, 'You'll want to see my horse.' The Moon wafted around the cave, resplendent as she went. 'Here it is,' said Grinder at last, standing hand on hip, 'my lovely horse that I've created just for you.'

The Moon

Grinder saw her pause, retreat a little, perhaps, and take a second look. The night sparkled. Perhaps she frowned. His spine shrivelled. Grinder felt himself begin to sweat.

Then she spoke, or so he thought, in a soft and mellow voice. 'Yes,' she appeared to say, 'He is a strong horse, with angry eyes and mane. He speaks to me of blood and war.'

'Yes, yes, and killing,' said Grinder, clenching a joyful fist. 'He does, indeed, and death. Do you not think?'

But a disappointed quality had crept into the voice of the Moon, 'I see you have another creature,' she said, smoothly shedding light on Gimlet's painting. 'I say,' she shimmered, 'whose horse is this?'

Grinder coughed. 'That's a practice one knocked up by my sidekick, Gimlet. He does a bit of sketching. It's not what you would call –'

'I think it's excellent,' said the Moon. 'Where is this Gimlet?'

'I'm over here,' said Gimlet, from the shade.

'Oh, I like this horse,' she said. 'He is altogether a finer, more delicate creature than the other. Look at his noble head. His lines and neck. The length of his legs. The serenity in his eyes. He makes me think, tranquility.'

Gimlet climbed down from his perch. He stole a look at Grinder, without triumphalism, he hoped. He knew it was hard for him, but then, without hesitation, and in a moment of destiny, he simply tilted his head towards the Moon, ever so slightly, drinking in her presence, and, smiling like an enigma, he glowed as she repeated his name.

'This is more like it,' she said. 'What promise, you show, Gimlet, what sylvan subtlety.'

The Cuckoo's Call

Once, there was no House. Only a five-acre field belonging to McCafferty. A rising Meadow, with reeds, a view of the Sound, nothing near it and bursting with birdsong. Most mornings it awoke to the lap of shore water, to the gentle brush of a fox, to the tickle-tickle of a caterpillar foraging on sixteen tiny legs, on its way to becoming an Admiral.

Girls wearing starched linen brought muffins and butter. Spread rugs. Made lazy daisy chains, dreaming in the soft summer time of the deep long ago. Unaware.

Just an easy, any old meadow, it seemed, wanding catkins in February, waving slim branches to heaven, slender-waltzing in southern breezes. In August, hedge fruit hanging heavy in clusters. A wildness of garlic, a crimson of poppies. Cornflower returning each year, like swallows, in blue.

There were greenfinches and chaffinches, coal tits and siskins, all unaware. A robin's chiff-chiff patrolling the marches. Two cooing doves to gladden the heart of the Meadow. A visiting plover. A retired piebald horse, resting from the tramway, nuzzling grain from the clank of a bucket.

A brazen cuckoo arrived from Africa, fat, fecund, and plump, laying eggs in the nests of the warblers. It spent time with the Meadow, perching on boughs, sharing what it knew of the world.

The Meadow was no longer at peace. It had learned of tall spires, of sweet singing on Sundays, of clamour and children at play in the thrumming yards of schools. Of swift sidecars, the traps of gentry, the giant jibs of cranes. It had been stirred by the cuckoo's call, the flash of its imposter tail, imagining ships and gantries, scaffolds, rigging, and rum. It saw concrete mixers and mortar and stone-laden wagons standing in sidings, the ballast, ball bearings, hydraulics and torque, the propellers and steam.

The Meadow found it could not sleep for thinking of fine upright mothers and sturdy infants walking, of teachers and bright party games. Their capers, the sheen in their eyes.

Each day, and more and more, it languished for landscapes of brick that was hardened in kilns, for soffits, lead flashing, for gullies and drains. It lusted after iron window frames, for extending brass swivels, for closers and Bangor Blue slates. It yearned for strong rafters and bitumen felt, for the slant of warm sunlight streaming through panes, for the bend of bamboo, and the creak of cane chairs. It sought cool quarry tiles and the aroma of scones, a long breakfast room, marmalade, toast soldiers and tea from Assam.

It dreamed of herringbone floors, original oils, of young people swimming in the Liffey, the Lee or the Seine. Of mixed bathing, wind lifting hair, the lounging loose blouses of girls and their skins. It imagined the smoothness of distempered walls, of cherry and oak, of a spaniel asleep at a fire, a bakelite telephone, black as a cat in a basket.

'I want diffused lighting,' it said. 'Chandeliers, curtains suspended on cables, adjusted by pulleys and spinning steel spindles.'

It yearned for art deco, a bespoke ruby carpet bedecked with a frieze of darkest sloe, and a square of the most unusual lavender. It looked to the future and drooled.

An owl visits the Meadow, holding court in a candle-lit chestnut, each night. Hearing all, saying little. Fluffing his feathers, sharpening the curve of his beak. The Meadow sees that the owl is holding back. The Meadow says it wants debate, to have it out, but the owl does not heed cajolery, for it knows the ways of meadows.

'I need much more,' the Meadow says aloud, as twilight falls. 'This quietness is not enough. This peace is not my life. You must see that.'

The owl fails to raise an eyebrow. He does not scratch or flick a wing or do any of the things that owls are thought to do when meadows seek advice.

Instead, he makes low mewling, kitten sounds and travels behind his eyes to some faraway place. Each evening the Meadow speaks to the owl. Each time the owl says nothing.

Sometimes, around nine, the owl may make a thoughtful flight, scattering staccato squeaks of bats, crossing their parabolic paths, majestically snapping at midge swarms, flying beyond the boundary of the Meadow. Mice freeze. Voles peep in terror from their holes. A weasel wavers on his way. The fox growls. The owl flaps soundlessly. The Meadow breathes heavily.

The Meadow becomes fretful with the owl, grows hot beneath its sward. Distressed, it wants to leave this languid life. To revel in the subtle sing of words in wires, the deep, throat-throb of petrol-driven motorcars. It cannot rest, listening for the land rail's raucous crake, as night thickens with nocturnal creatures, and cities stir in sleep.

At last, the owl does not come back, knowing in his heart that the Meadow will go for topiary and manicure, for helmeted cavalrymen of crafted cotoneaster, grasping their razored reins.

Once, in an open moment, the Meadow had sought to give reasons to the owl. It had spoken with inflection. Syntactically. Pausing for effect, employing perfect punctuation, searching for a frisson of assent. The Meadow had taken heed of grammar and did not end a sentence with a preposition, arguing closely, and still the owl had simply blinked, refusing to give counsel.

The Meadow knew the reasoning of the owl but, in its mind, saw bowed apple boughs blossoming, Bramleys and fructive golden quince, Kemps and Russets brimming in bowls, a dappled wall for Conference pears on lattice and sweet-skinned purple plums. It craved azaleas, heathers, high privet hedges, thick glossy laurel, gunnera umbrellas growing gigantic by the brook, the fragrant wisp of lemon balm, flowering mahonia, a cultivated niger, two cypress trees to shade a green gazebo, a wooden shed, four canvas chairs, a fork, a rake, two pairs of gardening gloves, and so, it dismissed the unspoken wisdom of the owl.

The very day McCafferty sold the Meadow to the man and woman, a wicked storm whirled strangely from a cloudless sky. The pasture lost its lustre. Hail smote the earth. The horse could not get off its back. Sudden squalls peeled back the willow. The hawthorn hunched, lopsided. A searing gale took leaves and left bark bare. Spume clogged in nooks, clung to the Meadow's skin, spreading a shingle scab and everywhere a rash of filthy cuckoo spit. From the Sound a sudden whip of foam. Blisters furred branches of the elms. The rime of winter early.

The Meadow attempted to relax. It knew that change was tough. But in April came a deceitful birdsong. A frigid moon beamed hungry on the acres. The ground began to shake and tremors teetered trees. Below, a magma mantle moved. Above, frost chilled the souls of the man and woman.

The Meadow braced itself for the savage digger that would tear its scalp. It would be worth the pain. A happy house was on its way, spilling through turf, already formed, chimneys blazing. The digger shifted shale.

The House travelled at speed through the birth canal, slicken-siding and shearing rock. Now it stood steaming, fresh, as a new calf. Seasoned mechanics in boiler suits stepped forward cautiously, and wiped it down with rags.

The Meadow marvelled at the lines of the House, at the proud profile and elevation, at the pit below the double garage floor for men to work at engines. They carted off the afterbirth in dumper trucks. Boulders and aborted lumps of concrete to landfill, beyond the hill. Square loads of stones in Foden lorries. The thick glut of exhaust.

At first, the Meadow rejoiced in its good fortune. But the House had been thrust from the womb. It rested, a glassy glinting in its eye. It coughed to clear its pipes. It brought forth muck and mucus.

'This is to be expected,' the Meadow said, but trembled.

A progeny will have its way.

A mahogany table is laid. Coiled napkins cuffed in rings. Cut goblets from Tyrone. Franked silver. Claret decanters. The man and woman clink and chink, not fathoming the soul of the Meadow, not grasping the nature of the House.

They half smile and dine on Beef Wellington, poached apricots and brooding Cheddar cheese. The man goes to the library to read, the woman to her bridge. At times they climb the sweeping stairs and walk together, although apart, through high-ceilinged rooms with alabaster cornices, lingering longest in the nursery, a teaming jungle where tigers lie replete with meat and chunky elephants fly by, happy-flapping their trunks and ears.

They part Venetian blinds to study the mist, but smell the swirl of chlorine. They catch the gloomy glimmer projected by the lighthouse on the isthmus and listen to the gatling of magpies taking chicks. The shriek of black-backed gulls.

A handsome, well-stuffed teddy sleeps with eyes wide open. A fiddle hangs on a hook. A shelf of classics snoozes. A crafted wicker crib, and in the crib, under trimmed patchwork, at last, the soft breathing rhythm of a baby boy. Above his curls, like daggers, sharp-scissored shapes of clipped Matisse.

The woman paints with palette knives. Geraniums, wine roses plastered, thick.

The Meadow waits and hopes.

By the gate, Manus, their man, already in his dungarees, is at the boxwood – shearing, despairingly, with his ground-steel Spear and Jackson – combing its crew cut thatch with calloused hands, spreading blunt nicotine fingers, gathering twigs. Checking the lie. It's running off, he thinks.

Leeks, which the woman drops in holes, have swelled a maggot white. Savoys stay rampant, without their hearts. They hold a bitter tang. Raspberries come early, in unhealthy puffs, crucified, bloody, on cruel stakes. Coreopsis glows a sickly amber. The cistus is out of season.

Euphorbia bleeds a viscous milk, and rots.

The Meadow wants to talk, to learn its fault, but the House has turned its back. The baby's name is Boniface. Like Boniface the saint, murdered in 754 AD. After drinks, the man and woman entwine their bony hands a little and dryly kiss at times.

The Meadow sees it all.

The House has slaughter on its mind.

Boniface. 'A bonny baby, growing up,' the distant neighbours say. 'One day he'll be a skilful artist, like his mother, a young Picasso,' they tell her more than once. She finds her infant counting pebbles. A mathematician. Perhaps Brunel? A scientist?

Boniface splashes colours carelessly, mixing them to a mongrel brown or dun maroon. Dabbing at his page, idly. Stabbing with his brush. He does not care to paint.

Instead, he rides a reckless tricycle on rigid rubber hoops, rocketing in tight corkscrews, skid-marking the parquet, cornering crazily through doorways, scraping, slewing, skimming the aproned maid, upending her deep tureens of limp asparagus. Dead platters of cold cuts. Though he shuts his eyes for 'Grace'.

'For what we are about to receive…'

'Truly fankful,' lisps Boniface, so like a monk. An Anglican priest, his mother thinks. Religion has its place. Perhaps. Starched collar-stiff on Sundays, he stands, a boy soprano, reluctant under lamplight, tethered to his stall. The tug of rope. A single muffled bell. 'Gaudete' in December.

'A pleasant voice but weak,' the choir master tells the woman. 'His reading of notation is not, how would one say, precise? Sadly, his pitch can tangent off but let us see.'

His voice breaks badly at the age of twelve. He will, it seems, become neither a tenor nor a bass. A boy in no-man's-land, and therefore quite without potential.

The Meadow wonders.

The House cannot conceal its mirth.

The Meadow shudders and seeks the owl.

The woman strives with no success. The rhubarb twists and stunts. The tangerines she plants in terracotta, under glass, produce small galling fruits, sour tasting and the size of golf balls.

The man makes money. He joins Round Table, salutes the life size picture of the Queen, imports low-moisture wheat in bulk from Canada and bully beef from Argentina. He shoots in farmers' fields for sport and once he made an effigy to scare away the rooks. Boniface cried when they pecked its eyes.

The Meadow watches, helpless.

By day, an occasional neighbour sees the boy, lost and standing by a window, with the bear, whose name is Donger. No one knows why. At night, invisible in his world, alone, Boniface gazes at the firmament when stars are out. His father seldom sits with him and when he does, he stares at nothing.

Once, they invite that Ferris couple to walk beneath the pergola to admire the outline of the mountain. They ask for Boniface. 'He is asleep,' they're told. They have two children of their own.

The man and woman take a photo.

'How nice,' the Ferris woman says.

'Knotweed will be a curse. A rampant foreign scourge that needs eradication. Hogweed will consume the country, another canker. Rhizomes are the enemy, tunnelling like Germans, so to speak, if one may say that sort of thing.'

The woman smiles a troubling smile. 'This used to be a meadow,' she says. The Ferris couple shiver, but agree it is not cold. The clock ticks hollow in the hall. The Ferris man will, after all, drink a second glass of port.

Mrs Ferris wants to know if Boniface would like to come one afternoon to play with Jane and Frank. They have red setters and a goat that likes to climb in trees and stand lugubrious on hills, like Puck, and hens. The woman says that Boniface will be busy, practicing scales on their recently acquired piano.

They speak of commerce then, and shipping lanes, before the couple leave, speculating on the future of the Sound, of tugboat pilots, tourists and the price of land.

The woman sows lilies in her pond. She lays out lilac Russian sage and honesty, which she will doubtless dry in bunches. None of them take. The bees she keeps throw out their queens. The workers lay runts. Colonies perish in violent wasp attacks. She sterilises a pile of jam pots until they gleam, and boils a heap of damsons by the stone. She strains the must through several weaves of muslin and stores the spirit hot. Caps them with greaseproof paper and seeks to fend off mould.

Boniface will not excel at school. For years, he fears to leave the House and tries himself, on bleak, empty Saturdays, instead, at marquetry. He cannot cut or hold a pencil well. He does not draw. He lacks perspective. 'He will not practise,' the woman says aloud.

'He needs to understand the vanishing point when he's attempting boats,' a perspiring Mrs Reilly tells the woman, swallowing her Adam's apple.

His father has him coached in calculus. But his report is merely average.

'He does not see it,' his student teacher says.

He does not love to fire a gun and cannot club a rabbit on the head.

'When will he be a man?' his father says. Coronas make him retch, and billiards hold no allure.

The Meadow bleeds. It cannot find the owl.

The House stands back and leers.

Boniface begins to love fast adult cars. He wants to ride in Porsches and other powerful models. To circle Indianapolis on open, spoke-flash wheels. To lap forever. The man and woman talk. The House listens. The Meadow cannot hear. Boniface will kill himself. Come home incinerated, shrivelled like Takabuti, desiccated as a bag of coconut.

He dreams.

The Meadow implores the wind.

Boniface is working now as an under-manager in a paper mill, where a second language is not required, and Molière is quite unknown.

He faces a stretch of forty years under asbestos, in a corrugated hangar, by the shore, where spruce is churned to pasteboard and cartons shunt on eager forklift trucks. Someday he will have the house, the people say. He drives a company Ford.

The Meadow pleads with the House. 'We all can get it wrong,' it says, and other platitudes.

'He needs a girl with educated vowels,' the woman says, 'who eats politely and has an eye. Who knows the copper richness of photinia, a girl who owns an Astrakhan, is not afraid to wheel a pram through spray along the promenade. A tall young woman who likes to stride in home-knit wools and decent waterproofs, with no time for soft living, a wife to despise the ruinous effects of oil-fired central heating and rightly so.'

The Meadow hopes that Boniface will find someone to love, at least. 'We'll see.' So says the House.

Boniface's fiancé loves to dance. He melts. She shimmers. He buys a shawl in Meldron's to keep her creamy shoulders warm at Christmas. He calls for her in his Cortina. In June he motors the length of the peninsula, showing her off, stopping for beer when it gets hot. They play loud music in the car and jig the miles away. She wears a silky scarf and drives him wild. He sees her every night, for months, returning on his own, to lock the wrought iron gate, bouncing off cats' eyes, easing into bends, hugging white solid lines, ripping corners, drumming hard on asphalt. One night, on ice, he skews into a ditch.

He drives himself to be in time. In time to lift the labelled keys and turn them in the padlocks twice, like he was taught. To snap the brass protectors shut, to keep the water out. Each night, at twelve, he dashes between drumlins, too fast, too fast, drifting dangerously, testing the treads of the Ford, straining its hidden track rod ends, reaching the House, to close it up and slam the bolts.

The Meadow admires his choice but she does not please the woman, or the House, who finds her 'Tinkly'. Cheek bones too high. Her kohl too bold. Her hair too blond, nail paint too red, her lips too full. 'No knowledge of the flora,' the woman tells the man. A girl without respect for aphids. Who has not sprayed with Derris Dust and has, lamentably, in all probability, a mother who is stout. No, she will not do. Boniface lets her go. His head is down.

The Meadow appeals to the air.

The owl has gone.

The House is adamant. 'You brought me forth without consulting me,' it says. 'I pass on pain. That's what I do.'

Boniface now begins a frantic swinging of his scythe, a wild snatching with a bill hook, a constant burning of bonfires, of smudge smoke and splintering wood. He madly mows until the Suffolk Punch is jammed with grass. He clears the blades, bare handed – no Manus now – adjusting screws. He yanks the cord a dozen times. He swears and sweats and mulches beds, he rakes the tilth, and feeds camellias bags of ericaceous nutrient. And yet, they do not thrive. He slices suckers from Floribunda and tops three kinds of dogwood, working by flashlight with secateurs. He squeezes cutworm to make them burst and squelch, and sprinkles salt on slugs.

The Meadow looks on, helpless.

Boniface rises at six, alarmed, without a clock, to bake for the man and woman. He makes them broth from marrowbones and lumps of shin and brisket.

The woman and man grow stiffer. Boniface works faster, clambering higher on extending ladders, dropping plumb lines to get an edge, taking longer over less, pulling muscles in his legs and chest. Lopping thicker limbs from trees with electrical contraptions. One day he nicks the soft place on his arm and makes it spew.

The Meadow moans.

The man dies.

The woman lives inside her skin, sinewy and slack. The nurse who calls to take her blood can never find a vein. She taps and taps.

'Blue saggy little eels,' the woman says. The walls are weak. At last, the phial fills.

'My veins are flaccid, Boniface,' she says.

But she has kept her teeth. He brings her Spanish anchovies and Lunns' scotch eggs. She keeps the sausage meat and spits out shreds of albumen. He shops in Frankie Farrell's on a Wednesday for ripe bananas, and speaks to no one, nodding silently.

He buries her with mildewed hymns. No flowers. Their dog-eared vicar has a bout of flu. He mumbles through his nose. His morbid words dissolve. 'Dust to dust,' he says, and not much else.

The House is cheered.

Boniface is a broken man at sixty.

The House looks on. It's a guttering fridge. All shrouded in drapes and calico.

He eats from tins.

A stranger he encounters in the doctor's surgery, tells him that he should move. 'Downsize,' is the word he uses. He can't. He won't. He has the House to think of.

He strains to row his boat, caught by an unseen current. Waiting, played out, at the end of his hawser. Now on warm evenings, he seeks a faded deckchair and takes a cushion from the breakfast room to ease his neck and searches for lights across the Sound, myopic. He has done his best with the House but it will not have him. He sees that much.

He drinks from one stained cup, loathing the thickness of delft, scooping, each morning, with a spoon, the porridge he's made the night before, ladling it, congealed in lumps, into his fissured mouth.

A new polished rector is at the door. He rings the bell but Boniface does not appear.

In Ferrys, amongst the bottles, the postman sips his Powers and says that the place is wrecked. He sees it as he passes with his bag.

The Meadow smells death.

'It wants to reverse the clock,' the postman says, 'as if it could.'

'As if,' the drinkers say.

Buddleia and alders try to crack the tarmacadam. Birches prise gravel, but all without conviction.

When Boniface withers finally, a neighbour's daughter serves tea. He had it all arranged. They use the woman's Denby. Outside, men soak up rain.

A grand looking house,' they say, 'but it had no chance.'

'There was no call to build at all,' they say.

'It just took one.'

'Now there's houses everywhere.'

'The coast's away to hell.'

And on they go.

'Ah now,' they say, scuffing the alchemilla, 'another bugger is the Lady's Mantle.'

'What will happen to the house?' a stranger asks.

Petals flutter sadly from the fuchsia the woman brought back from Galway.

Four bleating undertakers hip-grind him from the altar rail, where he has lodged all night. They wheel him in his solid box of beech. He trundles slowly on the gurney, on its expanding criss-cross legs, to save their curved, bent backs. At the family pew they pause. It is truly vacant now. Its door is latched. 'The day thou gavest…' The organ's motor needs replacing. All money. Ah Boniface. A legacy. How kind of him to think.

Five choirboys flutter like kites, to see him off; to join the man and woman. The yews hold up stark arms.

From the east, rain pounds the earth.

Weeping is in vain, but the Meadow sheds tears for Boniface, for the world and for itself.

The owl flies low. It dips its wings but does not stop.

The House rejoices. It has just begun.

It will not forget.

Does not forgive.

Close at Hand

Kings Hall
that afternoon
on the
ice dodging there was
Welsh Lexie the Cardiff
cop who owned the van Toots
his forever French teacher
girlfriend expecting
the sparkler any
day her pen pal
mate Delilah why why why
Nookie Bring It On-McT and
Me-Spud from
Dublin in the
Green in the
Green.
Music
Lulu
Dusty
Tom
It's not unusual.

Atmospherics
art deco arches dry
reinforced choke in your
throat pure concave
baltic.
Breath
streaming
steaming.
Scarves
college long
stripes.
Smell
rubber sweat
two pairs of
socks.
Gear
blades hired red pom pom
hats wool
gloves.
Hormones
aplenty tall shaggy long-legged
freckled painted plain I
know that's sexist
now.
Drinks
fizzy Fanta orange no
beer no kidding
soft.
Couples
Toots and Lexie
Lexie and Toots.

Dolls
extra sexy Delilah out on her
own not for long scent
musk-mascara skating doesn't
need to busty beautiful that's
how it was back
then.
Skaters
nobody like Nookie for down low
skim finger-tip foot over
foot work hands
clenched behind his
back speed crocodile
lover of
Sheila who's not
from
Oz.

Me Spud
coasting without Molly
clichéd no
chance.
Action
Lexie sails past with
Toots smile-flashes
me smiles at
Delilah teeth
ivory at the
barrier.
Toots
doesn't love it Lexie's
idea she's just so
glad to be
his.
Nookie
catching Sheila he mouths she's
good.
The crowd
crow-flaps arms
slither.
The Ice
cut up and
scored.
Me-Spud
no Molly unsteady takes
Delilah out
intoxicated
overhauled by
Nookie and his

Shiela.
Delilah
only
gorgeous.
Sound system
Believe me
distorted.
Lexie
with Toots
Toots with Lexie.
Skating
Let's be having youse on
the ice.
The crowd
hacks round.
A dancer
in the middle
pirouettes.
Visual display
neon flash-happy
birthdays Mary from
Malone Debbie of
Dunadry.
Applause
applause.
Kiss
Debbie and Mary
shush.
The Ice
degrading.

Toots
slow gliding she's had
enough she
wants to
go.
Lexie
not yet takes Delilah out two
circuits.
Ice
clearing.
Dusty
you don't have to say you love me.
Announcement
crackles then silence please slow
drum
roll
drum
roll
every one
cheers.
Dusty
close at hand.
The ice
slush.
Slush
Toots
on her own.
Announcement two
boys and girls the engagement of
wait for it – I'm looking at T o o t s – she's
l o s t – at Lexie and Delilah.

Applause
applause.
Toots
Toots what is
it?
Delilah
smiles.
Delilah and Lexie
oh hell.
The van
the van.
Drum roll
drum roll
again.
Lulu
tell me like it is.
Toots
falls and bangs her
head blood
smears.
Nookie
slams in we lift up Toots.
Toots
doesn't scream.
Doesn't scream
Toots
doesn't scream.
Lexie and Delilah
gone
gone in the van.

Gone
Toots gone in the
ambulance blue
flashing
light.
The City
white coats Nookie his
Sheila Me-Spud no Molly with
Toots the teacher.
French teacher
Toots.
Toots
bleeds inside her brain. That's
bad.
Prognosis
poor.
Deceit
complete.
Me-Spud
did you see it coming?
Nookie Bring it On
the fall?
Me-Spud
no not the fall.
Nookie
Welsh Lexie the cop? Och aye.
I saw it
coming
a mile
away.

Bastards
Lexie and Delilah.
Music
I hope we live to tell the tale.
Me-Spud
Toots
Tom
she laughed no more.
No more
no more she
laughed no
more.

Smokes and Birds

Who was it said that you don't choose your parents? None of us would have picked our da, I can tell you that. Maybe your oul fella grew carrots, or built a fort for your toy soldiers or took your mother a spin in the jam jar? Not our da. He was into pigeons and tobacco. Ma didn't count. She said she was allergic to feathers, and up until his accident, that was the only thing he conceded. With a bad grace. 'I'll never be happy without birds,' he said, at least once a day.

Da was a total spoofer. The Queen had waved at him, once, from her car, outside the pork factory, in 1953. Oh aye, and he'd nearly won the pools. Ma had distracted him that time, when he put in Everton instead of Wolves. Da was supposed to be best mates with champion dog breeders, and spivs that could get you stuff. We got nothing, sweet F A. He knew everything and Ma knew nothing, because Ma was a woman and she couldn't help it.

'Ciggies don't give you cancer,' Da said, filling his lungs. 'They're good for your brain. Well-known fact.' His brain definitely needed help. There were six of us. Other people's das beat them up for smoking, but he fed us fags like Haliborange. Everybody in the house smoked, except Ma, so we never had nothing and Ma got emphysema anyway.

'Suck on that, Son, it'll calm you down. Look at our wee Tommy,' he said, 'stick a duncher on his head, and he's a dead cert for Mackies.'

Mackies was heavy engineering.

'I hope he'll bring in more money than his da,' said Ma.

Tommy threw up on the linoleum.

'Mop up that bloody mess,' he said to Ma. And she did, for a long time.

His great friend Weed agreed with everything he said, and at the start, he was never out of our house. 'I keep telling you, Weed, don't be knocking the door,' Da said, 'come on, on in. You're one of the family, so you are, isn't he, Sadie?' Ma shrugged. That would be him and Weed for the night, smoking and being waited on. Weed kept pigeons in his roofspace.

'I'd love to go and stroke them,' Da said. But he never did. Just held it against Ma, and stayed in.

Coughs travel down the years. I can hear her still. We never knew it was the smoke at the time. Poor Ma. She used to repaper the kitchen but it was a waste of time. In the end she gave up. New skins of nicotine formed quickly, till the walls shone poisonous all over again.

'See if Sadie had've smoked,' Da said, 'I wouldn't have looked at her.' Women's lungs weren't made for smoke.

'True bill.'

He hated her going out. 'What the hell do you and that Elsie one have to yak about?' he said. Elsie was her one friend.

He kept the racing on at Goodwood, with the sound turned down. We couldn't remember him working. The 'oul sciatica' had floored him, so it had. The pain was, 'Shocking. Second only to gall stones,' – which he'd never had.

Childbirth, of course, didn't count in the pain league because it was 'natural'. Ma knew all about that. Breeches, sections, induced labours, you name it. He never so much as lifted a cup. Sometimes he beat time to the wireless. 'Open a tin of spam for us before you go, Sadie love,' he would have said. Ma worked at a laundry, boiling up dirty sheets and real working men's shirts. Scourging her two arms red. Standing stewing all day in steam.

'How does she stick him?' we said.

'She had to marry him,' said Lizzie, 'or Mary would've been a bastard. Wouldn't you, Mary?'

The Beatles were singing 'Help'.

'Bastard's a bad word,' said Joanie.

There were the two wee ones, as well; Freddy and Tommy, who had also been accidents.

Sometimes us older ones played records in the poky front parlour, but Da was always banging the wall and saying it was shite. Ma and

Elsie went to the bars on a Tuesday night. Women weren't supposed to drink, but it was desperation.

One day Da came home from the bureau. 'Bloody hell,' he said, letting on there was a mystery, 'they're sending me to a job.'

Ma was wetting herself, but it was true.

'Night watchman,' he said, like a lord mayor. 'It could be worse. At least I'll have time to think.'

We couldn't get over it.

'Maybe you'll write poetry forbye,' Ma said.

'It'll not be like working in a warehouse,' Da said, 'I'll be able to get a smoke.'

Weed called. 'Great news,' he said, when he saw how Da was taking it. 'I'll come and stoke your brazier.'

'With coke,' Da said, suddenly an expert on fuel.

'You'll have a wee hut, and all,' said Weed, 'and a bloody great hurricane lamp.'

Ma gave it a week.

It was hard to fathom but Da seemed to take to it. He hummed when he headed out at six, with his good dinner in him and his piece under his oxter, like a proper da. 'Did you put cheese between them digestive biscuits?' he asked her. He was taking no chances. A man needed strength to doze the night away. And he had his fags.

We went to see him once. There was a good going fire in his pig iron basket. It was shimmering a volcanic orange and there he was, inside the roll-along, with his coat on, studying the naked women in *Titbits*, and sucking in smoke.

'You should get a job too, Weed,' he said, 'nothing like it.'

But Weed said, 'Nah, too much on with the birds.'

'Oh aye,' Da said. 'I forgot.' But he hadn't forgot.

They were laying pipes on the site where Da was. He was an expert on building now. 'People don't know what goes on under the ground,' he said, 'before they can lay one solitary brick. There's a city of sewers down there, below the city, and if it wasn't for me, every damned thing sitting on the site would walk.'

Ma had a fry-up ready for him coming in. Each weekday morning she stood at the gas, cracking eggs, and the hot fat spitting at her, keeping herself late for him.

Then one morning he didn't show. She'd left his rashers in the oven with a note on the draining board, and gone to the laundry. He didn't come home that day or the next, because he'd been clobbered on the head with a lead pipe by the gang who took the compressor and a whole rake of tools. He told us that he'd, 'Sliced one of the hoors with a spade.' We knew rightly. The day-men found him in his donkey jacket, with a dent in his head. For a while he sat about like a dog in a muzzle, clamped up with the wires and bolts that held his skull together. He'd been taken to the Mater: 'The nurses were beautiful, but there were too many holy pictures.'

That was when things changed.

For a while he couldn't move his neck. Weed sat with him, in a wilted sort of way.

When he started speaking, his words were slurred. Blood had leaked in his brain and dripped to somewhere, like oil. It had to be reabsorbed. We almost felt sorry for him. 'Feel my head,' he kept saying. 'Put your hand in it. Aye, there.' We'd never touched him before.

Ma watched him with her bright eyes. It was hard to say what she was thinking.

Da learned to walk again between smooth parallel bars. White knuckled, he stumbled his way into the future. He was always looking for Ma now, but in a different way. He was a big awkward toddler. Not wanting her to leave him.

Ma seemed to be changing too. She brought him Mansize Kleenex and a hundred Gold Flake. They let you smoke on the wards then. But he didn't want them. 'Take them away to hell,' he said. This was Da – refusing smokes. 'Give the whole buckin lot of them to – what's his face?'

Ma looked at Mary. 'Weed's your best friend, Da,' Mary said, 'and you can't remember his name.' Neither he could.

'What would I want with a glipe like him,' he said, 'and my head opening. The doctor said he'd never seen a worse case.'

'In the entire world,' Ma said.

'That's right,' he said.

Da still sat around, but now he cried – for his mother, in a strangled way; for nothing; for just being alive.

'Do you want a fag, Da?' Tommy asked, with two in his mouth. 'I'll light one for you.' Tommy was seven. He didn't get it.

'Walk me to the corner, Sadie,' Da said. It took them an hour, there and back. Now he would smile at her like a wee fella, and lift a tea towel to dry the dishes. He yanked the handles off as many cups.

'You don't have to,' Ma told him. The whole thing was crazy.

I heard her on the phone to Elsie. 'No, darling, I can't,' she said. 'He's like an Elastoplast.' Da was. He followed her about. She called him her shadow, but she was holding it together, and we admired her.

'He keeps dragging me off to bed,' she said to Elsie, 'he hadn't been bothering me before.' I wondered what Elsie said.

The job was kiboshed.

'"I have to give you the beg. I don't want to, but my hands is tied." That was the boss. And here's the doctor, "You're going to be an invalid now, you might as well get used to it."' Da's eyes welled up.

Our Mary had a wee boy, right enough, called Shane. She and her man, Wullie, weren't married, and Shane wasn't his but Wullie took to him. Da had never actually hit us, but now we had to watch him with Shane. He was all right a lot of the time but he would take the odd crack at him.

He still didn't like Ma going out, and now he'd hardly let her out to her work. He got himself worked up over nothing and thought she was doing a line. With Weed, I mean to say. 'Do you see if I catch youse together,' he said, 'I'll put him in a box.' He traced the shape of a coffin with his fingers. He could still do that.

Ma was like somebody working out stuff in her head. She pretended to go to church to get a bit of peace. Da set the alarm clock. He asked her what hymns they'd sung. He wouldn't go to the handicaps club in the community centre.

Our house was draughty, but he wouldn't let us close the door. 'I need to keep an eye out,' he said. People walked past and pointed. It was like living in the zoo.

Mary took Shane away. Moved in with Wullie. Tommy started wetting the bed again.

I asked Ma, straight up, 'Why did you marry Da?'

'His body worked then,' she said. Nothing makes any sense when you're a child.

The compensation cheque was a pale pink colour – like the lupin we had in a pot before it died – with a squiggly black signature at the bottom. We'd never seen a cheque before. Ma held it up and kissed it.

'Sign you the back of it,' she told Da, 'and I'll put it in the post office.' Da gripped the pen like Sooty with his wand. It kept slipping but Ma was patient.

'It will be all right, Bertie,' she said, 'just take your time.'

He kept saying, 'Fuck,' and, 'I was a good writer once.' His head seemed to be getting bigger, like it was swollen but you think all sorts of things when you're young. Drops of sweat would glisten on his scalp.

The next thing was, out of the blue, she bought him a yellow budgie. You should have seen him.

'Awk, a wee bird,' he said, shaking his head. More tears. 'It will be nice and warm to hold.'

Mary said his Ma hadn't loved him. She wouldn't tell us how she knew.

Ma said the budgie would lift his mind. It kept saying, 'Help, help me, Rhonda,' and he kept laughing.

'Listen till it, he said. 'Listen till it talking.' His speech was coming on.

'Ah God, God,' he said.

'Well,' said Ma, 'he's not smoking now. It's the only pleasure he'll have.' We didn't know what she meant at the time.

The budgie was called Craig, though it turned out to be a girl, because it laid a wee egg. He played with it non-stop, coaxing it on to his finger and letting it climb on his bald head. 'He likes my dinge,' he said. He gave up the racing. 'That bird has more sense inside its skull, than them buck eejits in that box,' he said. So, the TV stayed off. I didn't care but Tommy bawled.

One day Da hit Ma hard in the face, but she said he wasn't responsible. Then he hit her again. She said she didn't want a fuss.

That was the start of it. The more he punched her, the more she kept bringing in birds till the living room was like a pet shop.

There was no doubt that Da had changed, and so had she. She didn't even seem to mind cleaning up the bird shit. And her allergy hadn't played up. Maybe it was only pigeons that affected her. But we wondered. She was like a soldier looking on the bright side.

Da told her he wanted more room for the birds. 'It's not fair to themuns, Sadie,' he said, with his voice all choking. 'They're all on top of each other.'

Ma smiled and said she knew.

One evening I saw her studying his face for a long time. Taking in all the lines and wrinkles of the years. 'We could probably afford to build a proper place for them in the back yard,' she said, 'with the compensation, if you'd like.'

'Oh aye,' Da said, 'that would be a slap on the kisser for your man.'

'Your man' was Weed, his used-to-be sidekick 'That would be dead on, Sadie,' he said. 'I'm telling you, come here and sit on my knee.'

'God save us,' said Ma, 'I'm not sixteen.'

'You're still my girl,' Da said.

Ma didn't hang about. 'We'll do better than Weed,' she said, 'we'll have a proper bird house.'

We saw a new side to Ma. She nabbed her nephew Ivan, the big, blonde giant, to draw a plan. She was talking like a joiner, in square feet, and about screws and mineral felt. Her and Da would be getting plenty of fancy birds from Bolivia and Zanzibar.

'I hear you,' said Ivan.

'Ha, bloody ha,' she said. She wanted high level cupboards and a Belfast sink for washing feeders and an electric plug for a heater, to keep them warm in the winter. 'For God's sake,' she said, 'it's money well spent. Stick in a neat wee toilet, Ivan, would you, while you're at it?'

Ivan was some worker. She went out the back and handed him tools. One day we heard her and him singing some oul come-all-ye. They weren't far apart in age. Tommy collected the off-cuts to play workmen and there was a powerful smell of resin.

'Put a good door on it,' she said, 'his birds will be worth a fortune. We don't want them being stole.'

When the bird house was finished, we all went out the back to christen it. Ma and Da and the whole six of us, Wullie and wee Shane came over specially. It was the first time I remembered us being together to admire anything. We drank a lot of Coke. Ma had a bruise on her cheek, but she was looking happy. It was a bloody good job.

'They're going to love it,' Da said, running his hands over the perches for the bird's feet. 'It even has a bog,' he said, jooking into the cubby hole where Ivan plumbed it in. He gave the chain a yank. Water gushed into the bowl. 'Like a waterfall,' he said. 'I hope the birds will use it.'

'They better,' Ma said, smiling at Ivan. Smiles have a lot of layers.

Da went round every bit of it, testing the wire for tightness. 'They'll not get out of here in a hurry,' he said. 'Friggin' Weed'll be green when he sees it.'

'Sure, you're not speaking to Weed no more,' said Mary, holding on to the wee lad.

'I know,' he said. 'I'm only saying.'

'It's like Carrick Castle,' I said.

'Aye, Son,' he said. 'It's here for keeps.'

'Aunt Sadie's specifications,' Ivan said, laughing.

'Sadie is a clever woman,' said Da. 'I never knew she was as smart. Can we have a photo, to remember us? Get you thon wee Brownie,' he said to me, 'and give it to your man, there.' I handed it to Ivan.

'All of youse stand in,' said Ivan, 'and say "Pheasant."'

'I'm not the pheasant plucker,' said Da, 'what the hell?' It was like a party.

'Do you know what I'm going to tell youse,' he said, patting Ma's head, 'this one has been the making of me. I wouldn't be here today without her standing by me.'

'That's enough,' said Ma.

'No, I mean it,' he said. 'Maybe I wasn't always, what do you call it, to her but I want youse to know' – big plopping tears – 'how much I love her. Sure would youse look at this here, now.'

We stood in front of the bird house. Ivan clicked the Brownie, catching us forever in monochrome, the day that Da loved Ma. It was all too much.

'You can ask Weed round now,' he said. 'I want to rub his face in it. Many's the woman would have buggered off, but not my Sadie.'

'God's sake,' said Mary.

Ma was on a different level. Her mind was running sweetly. Ivan had built in a long bench against the wall, wide enough to lie down on.

Da sat down on it. All of a sudden he was knackered, burned up by the excitement.

We stood and admired the bird house, smoking and breathing in yacht varnish. Then Tommy went into it and let on to be a chicken, running about and saying, 'Cluck, cluck.' He strutted up and down inside the wire, pulling faces.

'Would you look at that wee fool?' said Da, waving in at him and giving him the fingers.

'You have all your orders now, Bertie,' said Ivan.

'It will do me my day,' said my da.

It was like something had gone off in Ma's head.

'Get out of that, our Tommy,' she said.

Ivan held up a big brass padlock and a key. Da reached out his hand. It was pale and crinkly, and shaky, he was that overcome.

'Give that key to me,' said Ma. 'You would only lose it, Bertie.' I watched her counting out the green pound notes for Ivan. 'That's it,' she said, handing him the bundle of cash, 'whatever you say, say nothing. There's a bit extra there for the… all the bother.'

Ivan grinned. He kissed her on the cheek.

'Good luck, Aunt Sadie,' he said. 'I hope it all works out.'

'Oh, don't you worry,' she said, 'it will work out.'

We couldn't wait to see the birds flying in their new home but Da was in a daze. 'It's a great job, Sadie,' he said. 'It will be the quare man. When can we put the birds in it?'

'We'll have to see,' said Ma, 'tomorrow maybe.'

I'd never felt sorry for Da before. I'd always cheered on Ma. But now when I saw her with him, I wasn't sure. I watched her slide the key into her apron pocket and pat it, and I had the strangest feeling in my belly, a feeling of having learned a whole lot, and of never really knowing anybody.

'Nobody touches this key,' said Ma, 'are you all listening. I mean it. Not anybody.'

One Mother's Love

Kenneth Speck's story, told in his own words, in conversation with our crime correspondent, Henry J. Crabbe at HMP Limewood, 1979.

Poor Mother. She wasn't the same after father passed away. Funny how we've dropped the 'away'. Have you noticed? Now we just pass. Pets pass too. That's another change. Dogs and gerbils. Even my goldfish passed. I said 'goodnight' to my finny friend – there he was, swimming in his bowl – and in the morning, he was gone without a by your leave, floating on his side, all rubbery, the way they do, and he'd passed.

He was a tall man, was father, in his prime. We lived at 13 Weston Street. He bought it from the council when he was still climbing without a rope. He was a brave man. Ropes were for pansies, though he wore his protective glasses when he drove the combination – that's a motorbike and sidecar. 'It's the eyes, Kenneth,' he told me, 'you have to watch the eyes.' We had a tiny, front garden with those daisies that smell of pee and an ash that wouldn't grow – 'Stunted,' father said. We weren't in the town but we weren't in the country either, 'not properly,' according to Mother.

Father was a steeplejack. Do they still say that? 'Oh, he lives in the clouds,' said Mother. For a while I thought he was an angel. He had plenty of nerve but no time for banks. 'No, no, they take your cash and give you nowt.' I'd say he had the second sight. Do you believe in that? Folk seeing in the future.

'I'm laying some by for you, Kenneth, son,' he'd say, 'for when I'm gone.' You'd have thought he knew. He kept it in an old pottery egg crock under the stairs, where we popped the hyacinths to bring them along. Dark it was, and reeking of organic matter. There was a kindness in Father, when you saw him.

They're never the same, though, after, are they? The old ones left behind. In couples. I know Mother wasn't. I suppose you'd say that death was a bit hush-hush then, like having TB. You didn't talk about it. It was like ripping a jumper in two – not that you would, but say you did – neither bit would be any good. Anyway, there was father, after his tumble from St Joseph's spire – did I tell you that – lying in the graveyard, on the hill overlooking the chimneys of the mills, no use for anything, and Mother was coming apart. 'Unravelling,' she called it, 'all those loose stitches, purling like the branches of a corkscrew tree, twisting and going nowhere.' That's what she said, more than once.

'Mother,' I said, 'you're unconnected, and you're too thin.' She was too. 'Pasty,' I would have said, 'I don't like the look of you, Mother.' I meant no harm. It was her colour, like cardboard, or the fish she fried in Trex. I said, 'To be honest, you look grey and she said, 'Don't, Kenneth.' 'Mother,' I told her, 'you've got to eat.'

I was glad, though, when she went back to bingo. I could walk the greyhound again with an easy mind. I had hopes for Lady, once, but she caught her paw in a trap, just after they were banned. We had a lot of vermin from the river, mice and water rats. She was lame for years, like a three-legged stool, she was. I hadn't liked to leave Mother, you see, on her own at first, after father – well you don't, not after a bereavement.

It was bracing to get the air. I'd just had my birthday. I was forty. I'm nearly a pensioner now. I remember she bought one of those arctic rolls in Kerr's, and we shoved a candle in the middle. Eh, but I loved the jam and sponge with the ice cream. *Birds*, I think it was. 'Life has to go on,' I said to Lady. I said the same to Mother.

We were on the pig's back for a while, the two of us. She was seeing her pals again, little Amy and Polly Hampton and Smoky Pam, if you've heard of her, all wheezing together on their Woodbines in the Legion. One day she won a bear. It was only a toy. She carried it home in the green bus, without a wrapper. Mother said the conductor smiled. 'I'm sure he did,' I said. 'A drunk man asked me if he was a teddy boy,' Mother said. '"I don't know, I'll look and see,"' she told him. That's what she said. Oh, she laughed at that, did Mother. I laughed myself. And he was a fella, right enough, because she called him Stanley, after father. He was overstuffed and had a wonky eye hanging loose on his cheek, a glass ball on a piece of string, looking in all directions, like someone had gouged it out. We kept him on our two-seater, the one with the flat nail heads and wooden arms that she bought from the Clarkes when they sailed to Australia. They couldn't take it with them. It was a good buy because me and Mother had our own chairs for watching *Coronation Street*. I sat on the right of the bar heater, under the three ducks – 'Where are they flying to?' I asked, when I was little. 'God knows,' she'd say – Mother preferred the seat at the window, by the geranium. We were cosy then.

Nobody ever called, except the regulars, on a Friday night, looking for money with their little black books and stubby pencils. The breadman was a strange chap that used to be a nudist. Jimmy the milkman wore those knitted gloves with the chopped off fingers, oh aye, and there was a freckled window cleaner by the name of Fergie. Once a month he left religious tracts. 'Flee from the wrath to come', is one that I remember. With pictures of flames. I can't say it brought me comfort. We called him Shammy – people get to look like what they do. I knew a cook, one time, called Bacon. He had a flat face, did Shammy, from pressing tight against the panes. He was a nosey bugger, always trying to catch a glimpse of Mother's corsets and underthings. 'Like George Formby,' Mother said. I can see him now, Mr Crabbe, right as rain, his bucket swinging, plonked on his short, pointy ladder, shirt tail flapping like he's pegged on a clothesline. We had a fishman too – everybody was a man – with a cold, blunt face. 'I do wish he wouldn't whistle,' Mother used to say, 'it so reminds me of a corpse.' It was an odd way to put it really, but she meant no harm. Mother had her own expressions. 'There he goes,' she'd say while I rummaged for his two shillings, 'whistling, like a dead man.' 'He'll hear you, Mother.'

Her favourite was Betty Turpin that pulled the pints in the Rovers Return. Do you remember Betty? 'I'd like to have a bun like hers,' she said, but she never did. I didn't ask her why. Well, you didn't, with Mother.

The first thing I noticed about Bob was his big red hands and matching ears. Bat ears, they called them, like he only needed to waggle them and he'd fly – Big Ears, do you remember him and his chum, little Noddy? – only with bits chewed out, like a ferret had been nibbling. I'd just come in, with Lady, from the dams. She liked a scamper though she looked right silly. Poor old girl. 'The rabbits are laughing at you, Lady,' I used to say. I'd always liked a dog.

Bob was in my seat. He was not a big man, not like father, but he was heavy looking and he filled it. 'No, don't get up,' I said. He had no notion of rising. He was drinking tea out of the china cups we bought in Filey, Mother and me. We'd spent a week in mackintoshes, licking cones and sitting in chip shops, watching the seagulls through steamy windows. They made ever such a racket every morning, at the B&B. 'You have to have gulls, Kenneth,' Mother said, 'when you're at the seaside.'

She'd given him a Wagon Wheel. They were called 'The treat for me' on telly, and they only ever cost tuppence, or was it thruppence? But they got smaller. She'd taken it from our secret tin with the picture of the Duke of Edinburgh. She loved the Queen better, like we all do, but the day she bought it there was only Prince Philip's left. 'He sleeps with the Queen,' the man said, 'that's close enough. I'll let you have him cheap.' I could see Bob's teethmarks in the mallow.

'This is Bob,' Mother said, her own teeth clacking. They were loose, you know. I said, 'Oh aye.' She'd got him at the bingo. He didn't speak then. Not much, any road, but he stared at Mother. Folk said she were a nice-looking woman before she smoked. Now, I smoke myself, in here. There's not much else to do. I thought he was one of those dafties, though you didn't see them out much then. And why would Mother want one? But he wasn't daft. 'Bob's my friend,' she said. 'He thinks I have a lovely home.' 'I imagine he does,' I said. We had a front room and a larder.

That was the beginning of it, I can tell you. It was Bob, Bob, Bob. I said as much to the ginger fella at the Labour Exchange – I'd known him for years – I told him I couldn't sleep. 'Mogadon,' he said, 'and I'd watch him if I was you.' He had an odd way of closing one eye, like Stanley. 'He'll be on the make,' he said, filling in the form for me. He was good that way. 'That Bob owned petrol pumps,' he said, 'and he's been married twice. He has two cottages in Wheatly. He got them from his wives but they're both gone, RIP, say no more,' he said, the way country folk do, raising an eyebrow. I never could. Wink, that is. I said no more but his words sat in my head like an egg under a hen, waiting to hatch.

It wasn't that I blamed Mother exactly or that I felt that much for father, but I don't like to see a man take the mick. I never did. And I worried for Mother. I said, don't interfere Kenneth. Let it be. It won't have legs, but it did, you see, oh yes, it did.

Bob brought her red gladiolas and a cheap delft clock. The kind you get in shops with sticks of rock and kiddies' Hong Kong chairs 'You don't grasp it, do you, Son?' said Mother, and she was right. I didn't.

All through the winter Bob came. He must have talked to her when I was out – I was out a lot by then – but what did they find to say? I was in by ten. After the weatherman, he'd down his cocoa and say, 'Well, that was a good cup, Mother.'

Mother!

'By heck, I must be off,' he'd say.

I never was fond of beer. It was water thin at first but I stuck with it, the way you do to be a man and I got on to it, in the 'White Rose'. Well, I couldn't cuddle up with them, could I, like some kind of extra?

'You're a right good darts player,' Joanne told me. She was the barmaid but she had a boyfriend, Tom Strong. 'Strong Tom,' she called him. They asked me to play for the team. We were known as 'The Bull's Eyes' after the mints.

'Don't fret, Kenny,' Joanne said, when I told her about Mother. But you do worry, don't you?

On Remembrance Sunday, we stood at eleven, Mother and me, in the scullery, our poppies held by safety pins, for the two long minutes thing. Do they still do that? We always did.

There'd been an early snow. 'Do you feel affected?' I asked Mother. 'Snow can make you sad.' I was thinking of the fallen.

'You can't forget the Somme,' she said. 'There was Dad and your great uncle David and young Alan Benson.' She'd been waiting for him, she said, lighting a lamp every night, but he never came home. He was shelled. Mother said she knew it was wrong, but after that, she'd always hated Turks. 'Slaughter-men,' she called them. I never knew if I was Alan Benson's or Father's. It would be one or the other, but I didn't ask. It wouldn't be fair to Mother.

Sometimes she reminded me of a tired horse pulling coal up Spindle

Hill. You could count its ribs. Her eyes were bright, like a haddock on a slab. Her legs, Mother's legs, were never what you might call, fleshy, but now they were lean, like butchers' bones. I didn't want to say. But I had to. You can't see your mother melt away, now can you? 'Are you weighing light?' I asked her. I thought I'd better. 'I've got things on my mind, Kenneth,' she said.

A week later, she and Bob were, 'Not getting married, surely, Mother?' I said it before I knew. But, aye, they were. She would be Mrs Steele. A different name from me.

'Bob's leaving me his cottages,' she said, 'at Wheatly. I'll leave this house to him, he'll look after you if I pop my clogs,' – it was a shock, you see – 'if I go first.'

'I don't think there was sex involved,' I said to the librarian when I changed my travel book. I can read a bit. I'd looked it up. She seemed surprised. She said she wouldn't know.

Mother or Bob would have three houses and me. I knew it wouldn't be Mother. I wasn't thick.

Bob was piling on the pounds. I noticed that. He was fond of sweets and fizzy drinks.

We'd never spoken of what they call 'end things', Mother and me. It wasn't done, but I went to see the Rev. Partridge at the vicarage. I'd never been to church, that I recalled. Only as a baby to be baptised, in case I'd go to hell. Mother said she'd never felt the need. 'Jesus forgave St Peter, after all, and look what he did.' The vicar was an Anglican. I liked the sound of Romanism better, with all their saints and smoke, or so I'd heard. He gave me pop and a whack of something stale, with cherries in on a plate. 'Do you know what I think?' he said, 'I think you should speak to Mum' – I'd never called Mother, 'Mum.' 'Talk to her about the house,' he said, 'on account of your being close.'

I couldn't. Not to Mother. I couldn't say, 'Are you really going to die, Mother?' or 'my but you're looking peaky.' That was a word we used. The vicar had a mournful face. His eyes were like sultanas and he had long fingernails like a girl, but I thanked him, to be polite. The way you do when it's all too late.

Sometimes, even before they were wed in June, Bob stayed the night. Mother said he should have my room, being a visitor and that. If there had been hanky-panky I would have heard when I was up with my bladder. I removed to the box room, above the hall, where it was cold. I drew stick men in the window ice. I didn't care. Mother said everything was sorted. 'If Bob goes first, we'll move to Wheatley.' 'But what if you go first?' I said, in the end. I had to ask. It was on my mind. 'I told you Kenneth, Bob will see to you, there's no one else.' Mother looked at me, like an old thin cow going to the abattoir in Binford.

'You'll be well looked after,' Bob said.

'He's a good lad,' Mother told him. 'In the bye and bye, he'll know it's for the best. He'll understand.'

But I didn't understand. I didn't understand at all. Well, you wouldn't. And I was not a good lad. I didn't want to hurt Mother but I couldn't live with Bob and what would I do with Lady? 'If he makes you happy…' I tried to say, like Ken Barlow, but I didn't mean it.

Such a summer it was. Grass catching fire from the steam engines and hose pipes banned.

I was what they call 'a witness to the marriage'. I wore short sleeves, and I went with a Miss Pondsworthy, I'm sure that was her name. She kept a dozen cats. But I wouldn't darken the 'Duck and Drake' afterwards for the steak and kidney. I couldn't face it. I told Mother I was glad for her. That she was the best mother in the world. I meant that bit. It made her weep and Mother seldom cried. All this talking. I'd like a drink of water.

One night Mother took a turn. 'Don't you think she looks awful?' I said to Bob, but he wouldn't let me go for Doctor Stone. 'She's doing grand,' he said, patting her like a second-hand car.

'I've got to do something,' I said to Lady. Every morning, I looked from Bob to Mother. At him shovelling his Shredded Wheat – it looked like straw – and Mother sitting, hunched in her house coat. He slept with her now all right. 'Just stay in the boxroom, sonny,' he said to me, 'why don't you?'

I did, but at night I prayed for Mother and myself. I lay on the canvas camp bed, with Lady beside me, and I swear, we prayed to God that He would do something.

I never had much schooling, but I was sure that Mother was finished. I kept thinking of St Brendan's, down in Eckton, with its high walls and the patients kissing in the grounds. I'd peeked in through the gate. I knew I'd be slipping five bob to Ferriter, like she had done for father, when he'd covered him with clay. 'I could never agree to cremation, Kenneth,' she used to say, 'I have a horror of the brimstone.' Poor Mother. I could hear the clods lumping down on her coffin, and the scrape of Ferriter's shovel. He was a great digger, was Ferriter, even in the heat. 'I'll be in Eckton,' I said to Lady, 'no surer thing.'

Bob would have to go before Mother, if you follow me, but I didn't know how. Do you know what I'm saying, Mr Crabbe?

Well, at first I went to the egg crock I was telling you about. It was full of spiders. A lot of legs, have spiders. I found nine hundred pounds in single notes. Mother had taught me how to count. It was a lot of cash but what use was it? I wanted to talk to her. She'd know what to do. But I couldn't, could I? Not the way things were, and when I thought on it, I didn't know any killers.

'Have you any murder stories?' I asked the woman in the library. 'Real or made up?' she asked. I knew 'made up' was 'fiction'. She thought that I was soft. 'I'm not particular,' I said, the way you do. I didn't want to raise a fuss. It was a small library. She gave me some large print books, the sort blind people use. There were pictures of axes and swords and they were full of electrocutions, gassings, stabbings and famous shootings. I liked them all but, when it came to it, I did Bob in with antifreeze. Aye, it was easier than I'd thought. I found it in the garage beside the tins of Castrol that father kept for his bike. Just the way he'd left them, as if he'd meant them for me, with his second sight and that. I love the smell of oil.

It was so hot that Mother asked Bob to buy a fridge. It stood in the corner, like a big tin cupboard, knocking on and off. Sometimes it shook, like Lady when she'd been in the dams. You could make ice cubes in it. I'd never seen ice cubes before. They didn't do them in the pub. I'm not sure if you know about antifreeze. It has a nice green colour, sweet. I mixed it with an apple drink I bought down in the Co-op. 'Pure juice is good for you,' the woman said. I took two bottles.

It looked terrific when I stirred it with a fork in our big glass jug. I poured a mug for Bob, like Mother used to do with Ribena. He was sitting in the scullery reading the *Mirror* and sweating in his vest. He drank it in one go. He had a great swallow, had Bob, I'll give him that. He crunched the cubes and wiped his mouth. 'By gum, Kenneth,' he says, 'that's right refreshing. What is it? It has a heavenly taste.' That's the words he used. He grinned at me with his eyes, like we were making up. He said I wasn't so bad. 'It's Ciderease.' I'd invented the name. 'It's new,' I said. He wanted more. 'No problem,' I said, like Joanne. 'Mother and I can't drink it, on account of our acid stomachs.' We were always sucking Rennies. 'Did you buy it for me?' Bob said and the next thing he's up with Mother, sitting on her bed, swigging it and telling her that he'll order a crate, if the heatwave lasts.

'I told you he was a good lad,' said Mother.

It must have been a couple of hours before Bob fell over. He had started a funny sort of gurgling and clutching at his belly and I said to Mother that he was poorly. She thought it was his appendix. 'Go next door,' she said, and so I did. Mrs Fulton was wearing a towel round her head. I could see down her front, but she rang three nines and in no time, they came for him, with the blue light going, in a big square ambulance that caused a stir.

Bob died that night. They say he died in pain. Mother said his organs must have failed. You can't live without organs. She took it bad, at first, did Mother. That was the worst of it. But then she said, 'He's gone.' We didn't say he'd 'passed'.

Four coppers swooped up from Binford, in their Morris. It had a lot of chrome. 'Look, Mother,' I said, 'it's the same as the Fultons'.'

I set a glass of Ciderease in front of me, to take them in, you know. Like in *Dixon of Dock Green*. Mother loved Jack Warner. I told them that Bob had been robust – I liked the word 'robust' – talking and swearing about the football, but then he took right bad. I thought I had them fooled but I wasn't drinking and they twigged. They'd seen it all before, so there we are. I should have thought of some other way, but I didn't have the brains. And you need experience, Mr Crabbe. Isn't that what they say, when you're looking for a job? It's been hard on Mother, though. I asked her if they'd hang me. 'They've just suspended hanging,' she said, 'I think you'll be all right.' 'But are you all right, Mother?' I asked, for I knew she'd be upset.

I believe in prayers now. Did I tell you? Mother got better. It was her gallbladder that was the bother. Nasty thing, a gallbladder. She'd gone all yellow. She said she'd felt like death. Poor Mother, she's come to see me, on the train, for close on fifteen years, in her light navy raincoat. Hell or high water, once a fortnight. She loves me. She doesn't blame me. 'God and the Queen's looked after me in here,' I tell her. 'I know, Kenneth,' she says, 'I know.'

She had to bury Lady in the garden ten years ago, by the dog daisies and the ash that never grew. She dug the hole herself. We'll have to let her be when I get out in August because Mother says we're leaving Weston Street. We're going to live in Wheatly. 'How will you get to bingo?' I asked. 'No more gambling for me,' she said. I didn't ask her why.

I've only been to Wheatly once. It had a post office then, and a drinking trough for animals, but I'm sure it will be grand. When I asked if we could buy a Collie pup, she sort of sighed. 'We'll see,' she said. She said it twice. But I know Mother. I've decided to call him Stanley. It's as good a name as any.

Kenneth Speck was released on parole after serving fifteen years of a life sentence for the fatal poisoning of Bob Black in the summer of 1964. He missed being hanged by four weeks and three days. Speck's words were recorded by special arrangement with Assistant Prison Governor Peter Barr.

Lost Tribe

Excerpt from Tales of Oakridge, *George Armstrong. First published by Paveroll and Sons, 1972.*

As a congregation, we held hard to the old ways of Catechism, Communion and The Ten Commandments. Like our planter forefathers, we walked, or at least we skirted, a narrow way through this wicked world. We neither smoked nor wagered nor took strong drink.

All my life I had lived for the First Ballyrammer Meeting House, both outside and in. Mending Wall, like Robert Frost, scything grass, repairing paths, tending the graves of the departed, whose souls would reclaim their Ulster bones on the last day. I had often climbed the steep slate roof to fix lead valleys and repair the flashing. I patched up floors and gave out psalters. Each Sabbath was a rekindling of who we were as we repeated 'The Lord's Prayer' and sang in parts. We had no truck with harmoniums or modern hymns. Let Catholics burn incense, and Anglicans flap in surplices, we worshipped soberly, in the good old way.

Perhaps we did not pray as much as we should have, but a more solid body of Reformed Calvinists you would have struggled to find. We held together like a separate people in a foreign land, not talking over much about faith, maybe, or even thinking a lot about The Holy Spirit, if I'm honest, but feeling mightily comforted to be stitched into such a sanctified remnant.

Denominations all have their histories and ours was the legend of a journey. In 1755, Reverend Robert Clarke, a former minister, in response to the aggravation of the times, led an odyssey to the New World where they could practice their religion unfettered by restriction. Great excitement is recorded amongst the Craigs and McCartneys, the Simpsons and my own clan, the Armstrongs, who had hailed from the Borders of Scotland before the Plantation of Ulster. With a will, they sold their lands and boarded the good ship *Resolve*, all bound for 'Americae'. A hundred and twenty soul – children, women and their menfolk – cast themselves on God's wide ocean and asked for a fair wind.

I'd often wondered how they fared, but their lives had been obscured by years. What we knew was, that when they reached Philadelphia, they travelled by wagon and made their home in a place called Oakridge, in Lincoln County. We could only dream of them sweltering there in the heat, singing and reading the scriptures in white wooden chapels, week in and out, the same as we did ourselves but in an American drawl.

Imagine then my surprise and delight, one Sabbath morning, when Willie Simpson, the senior elder invited me to the front of our plain meeting house to present me with tickets for a lifetime trip to the United States.

'In recognition of service to the flock,' he said. 'Go and seek out the good people of Oakridge and bring back tidings to our kinsfolk.' This was before all hell broke loose again in our afflicted corner of the island of Ireland.

I confess that I was moved to tears, for they had all contributed, and we were not a well-off group.

Accordingly on 3 May I crossed that self-same boiling Atlantic, not under sail, but inside a jet plane with four screaming engines. Having arrived safely, I immediately took a sleek Greyhound bus, which transported me to Oakridge.

Finding a small, rural community, I booked into the one seedy motel. Naturally, no one knew me. I asked about church folk over ham and eggs in a greasy café. The waitress wasn't familiar with any Calvinists, reformed or otherwise. From my cab, I had spotted a couple of tired-looking churches with weeds circling. I walked through town easily enough, past realtors' offices, as they called them, burger joints and billboards, searching for a respectable coffee shop. There were a lot of liquor stores. Young bucks cruised in rusty convertibles. It must have been a hundred degrees. I wasn't dressed for the heat and was forced to take refuge in some honkytonk place, for a Coca-Cola. Two men and a young woman in tight trousers twanged guitars, and sang, I suppose you might have said. All around the walls were pictures of steers and rattlesnake hunts. I can't say that I felt at home.

The woman said she was Bonny Armstrong. 'You have a request?' she called. It was foolish of me, but I joked and suggested the 'Old One Hundredth'.

'Is that Jerry Lee?' they asked.

After their set, they joined me at my little coggly table. 'You wanna Bud?' they asked. I had never been inside a public house. 'Everyone in Oakridge drinks,' they said. I laughed at that, but they didn't. She must have been a distant cousin, 'Maybe,' she smiled. I told them my mission but, they, 'Didn't do' religion. 'We'd like to visit the real Ireland,' they said, 'you know, with Guinness and, "Cute hoor music". Is that a genre?' They meant no harm. 'We know we're Scotch Irish,' they said, 'so, hey, maybe when we make it there, we'll give you a call.' They had heard of Bushmills whiskey. 'Go see the librarian,' they said. 'Maybelle knows everything about Oakridge. She's hot on folklore. You'll like her. She's kind of old school.'

On the outside, the library was a mean concrete rectangle. Inside it was an oasis of order. Maybelle wore a yellow bandana and round wire spectacles. She had long grey hair that tumbled in loose curls and a youthful eye. We had the place to ourselves. 'I'm just an old Dissenter,' I said, 'doing what you all do, in reverse.' I felt like an American.

Well, if she hadn't the greatest monochrome trail stretching from Civil War times. 'I've been working on an archive that might interest you,' she said. 'I don't get a lot of borrowers. It was laid down back in the early 1950s by Doc Rogers. Real life recollections, oral history, that sort of thing; mothballed, for years on magnetic tape. If you want an insight into some of your kin, you couldn't do better than begin right there,' she said. 'It's pure gold.' She looked at my dark suit and winked.

'Some of them probably became preachers – or presidents,' she said. 'But mostly they acquired land and cows, by… well pretty much any means they could. Just holler when you need me to flip the tape.'

Maybelle was kind. She set me up in an airless little room, with coffee on tap, and gave me peace. I was going to be a kind of eavesdropper. My heart was already bumping a little quicker. Thanks to modern technology, I would be joining with my own people. The tape machine hummed and I heard Doc Rogers say, 'Hi there,' in a homely sort of way, as if he'd recorded his stories just for me. Here is the first of those tales. I didn't intend to write it all down. I've spelled what he said, the way I heard it, so it's irregular and not the way we were taught by the master in Ballyrammer School. I particularly wanted to get the bits relating to church life in Oakridge. I was keen to have enough to tell the folks back home. In the end I transcribed the whole thing. In my head I know I was thinking of the Pilgrim Fathers, but they were English and they'd sailed a whole lot earlier.

The air conditioning had malfunctioned, but I didn't mind. My County Antrim bones were already drying out nicely, as I began to feel at home in this strange land.

Side One

'First, I want to tell you about Gretta, a friend and patient of mine,' said Doctor Elias Rogers. He sounded really intimate. 'She came from up river. Her daddy was supposed to have been hung but nobody knew for sure. She was staying in Oakridge above the saloon when I met her, playing piana and spilling outa her dresses at nite.

'That's when she fell in with Moses Gilroy.'

This was a surprise, but I let it roll... and roll.

'I was still married then. Moses was shaping to stay women-free, but she was a good looker an she had a way with her. He coulda give her ten years easy but she made a big play for him or else he wouldn't have been caught. It was before the Armstrongs took his land, otherwise she woulda moved her trade somewhere else. Gretta had already changed hands more times than a nickel when she hooked Moses.'

I wasn't expecting this.

'What's in the mind of a woman like that? I asked myself,' said Rogers. 'I'm still asking that question. Course he was a damned fool for being took in, but when a man's brain done slipped into his pants there's no talkin to him. He wants to be took in. I knew the feeling.

'Didn't have to wait long till he seen another, more real, Gretta, up close. The day they were hitched she threw a tantrum in the meeting house on account of some fool bunch of blossoms that didn't please her. She was fond of colour. Rev. Luther had to speak sternly to her about her language in the house of God, saying it wasn't no sawdust-spitting bar. Are people born to trouble, I ask myself, or does it grow in them like poke salad?'

I hadn't heard of poke salad.

'She was all flounces and tomfoolery from the start. I reckoned if it hadda bin me I would have sold her soon as I found a buyer. Though I wasn't reckoning on no line up. That's what I said, but how many men tells the truth?

'Wasn't much I coulda done for Moses's body, back then. He was swelling with arthritic pains on account of being out in winter weather, while Gretta's closet was busting its doors with new outfits, more than the Queen of Sheba. Some women need thrills and frills. A lotta men go for them too.

'How many do you know done the same as Moses? Judgement all messed up by smooth skin and bottles of face paints. Trouble was sure lying around the bend for him and worse than I'd seen for a long while. Gretta figured her life oughta been a whole bundle of vigorous living an having a good time. In their hearts, I believe, most folks are the same. She didn't make any changes on account of marrying. Which wasn't good, but I didn't blame her. Too many men blame women. She told me that bed-sharing with Moses didn't amount to a can of beans.'

No mention of church or God's plan.

'Thing was, unless she'd take pleasure in talking bout hens not laying, or changing a baby's diapers, there wasn't a whole lotta excitement for a wedded woman in Oakridge, with her juices flowing. And Gretta's were running like a river. Didn't take her long to work out she was strapped to a one-horse grubber. Life wasn't ever gonna come even close to the mark for no hot, full bosomed female. I remember thinking that.

'"Look at me, Doc Elias," she called me that, "you reckon the good Lord done designed a creature like me for dull?" I liked how she put it, but it struck me that more than a few thought it wasn't the Lord, but the opposition, that drew up her blueprint. If it was the Devil, I wasn't faulting him. If I'd had a tail, I'd have invented her myself.'

What do you do when something turns out so different from what you'd thought?

'There was no doubting but she had a sense of style,' said the doc. 'You'd have seen her mincing into town, high stepping like a pony, all airs, flashing the kinda smiles Moses never seen inside of a Christian home. A cathouse more like. Couldn't have been a day, when he took her out spend-thrifting, that he didn't dip his hacked hands into his pocket and pull out another twenty dollars and wish to God he'd never set eyes on her. It sure was a waste. Spending was in her genes. But he didn't complain. Told me he reckoned he'd done made a bed of rocks that he'd be lying on it for a mighty long time. He sure as hell was right about that.

'But Gretta brought with her an iridescence from someplace else. A kinda shining joy you couldn't describe. The day gleamed brighter when you saw her. Like when you swallowed a bottle of rye. Only better. A lot better. You might a called it a delicious wickedness.

'"Folks say I got sparkling eyes," she'd say to me, afterwards, buttoning her coat.

'"You think so?" I said. I was thinking on Moses's eyes burning in his head like dying orbs. It was awkward being in both their confidences.

'Gretta didn't have acquaintances among the women. No church wives stopped by to pray. Praying was going outa fashion. She didn't have nobody close, except me. Got no invites to baby showers. Too fond of men and showing it. Didn't pretend. Favoured staying acquainted with the male race at close quarters. Married or single, it didn't matter. Best shared secret in town. Dogs running the roads, red tongues lolling, woulda been in on it. Musta caused commotion amongst them, grinning and nudging? "Walter Withers left her like he'd bin give a bone, tail waving like Old Glory. Seen him cooling off at the waterhole." I knew the whole damned thing. Didn't make no difference to how I thought about her.

'Gretta didn't know the meaning of cooling off. Most every man between sixteen and sixty and some that was a whole lot more, had paid a visit to "Gilgall Ranch". That's the name she made Moses paint on a naked piece of timber, same time as the Armstrongs were pushing the bank to get him out. She brought a lotta happiness. Two hours of generous heaven when I could get it. Ain't saying I'm proud of it. Shit happens, but it wasn't shit. Moses was a good man and I knew it. She wasn't a bad woman. But hey, those were rare old times back then in

Oakridge. He musta known a helluva lot more than he was saying, like some of the prophets in the Bible.

'There weren't many saints walking about in Oakridge. He wasn't one either. Never used a holy word. Swore like the next fella when a sack of corn fell on him. Never knew him to quote scripture. No sign of a halo. He was just an honest mouthful of broken teeth, shovelling muck and trying to humour Gretta. Back humped as a camel, mind fraying like a rope at both ends. People said Moses's health was collapsing because he'd had to carry more than he should have. That was true. Wished I coulda make it up to him but I didn't wish enough. Had my share of carnality. He looked like the memory of a man that used to be.

'You know about respiration? You that's listening after all this time. It isn't something to spend a lot a time thinking about when your lungs are working regular, breathing in an out, sucking and blowing. Well, Moses had airflow obstruction. Maybe you've heard of that? It's like trying to draw air through a duct packed fulla straw and mites. You're swallowing and you aren't getting nothing except what's dry and killing you. I told Gretta she coulda took better care of him, but she said she'd give up. Said his gasping sounded like bellows that was eat by mice. I knew she was looking round her.

'Moses' place faced south. Woulda been a good aspect except he looked right into the Armstrongs' tumbledowns. Reminded him that cheating and stealing as a way of life, wasn't more than a mile away. The Armstrongs were born into it. Went back generations to old Pappy Armstrong. He wasn't a Mormon but he had three wives, and enough offspring to fill a haggard.'

This Doctor Rodgers was quite a character.

'I'm glad I'm speaking into this machine. Can't hold a pen so good these days. As I was saying, most of their territory they didn't have a right to, but they were always chipping away. Stole the biggest part of Moses' place. Challenged his title. Grabbed his best four hundred acres.

The scrub they left him wasn't worth a horse's ass.

'He woulda heard their mongrels howling at nite, smelt the stink of their livestock drifting on the wind, warm and sick. The Armstrongs were a tribe of savages. They came from some place in Ireland. They didn't patch no fences. Done everything like they were one big wolf pack. Moses said nothing about them, any more than he woulda complained about Gretta.

'Didn't have no time for doctoring, thank the good Lord. I never had to put a foot on their contaminated dirt. Nobody that went on their land felt safe. They weren't held back by thoughts of decency. They woulda took your rifle and shot you for passing wind. The Sheriff would sooner have shut a grizzly in the jailhouse, than tangle with an Armstrong.

'Moses and Gretta had reared two boys. First was Esau. Lightweight build and springy. Spoke sorta high-pitched. Used to go running in heavy boots to keep fit. Folks said he looked like me. Samson was slower moving. Broader. Nearer the ground. Solid, ankles to neck. Coulda hauled a harrow by himself. Growled when he spoke. Wasn't no similarity between them. Like a lot of kids in Oakridge, they never knew who their real daddies were. Their daddies wasn't Moses, that was for sure, but they sure as hell hated the Armstrongs, though their hands were tied because Moses didn't want no trouble, and the Armstrongs were well named. Wouldn't been any point in playing David and Goliath. Story like that only happens once.'

I needed a cup of coffee. But he was only starting.

'Neither Esau nor Samson stayed long at the schooling but they were known for their "ingenuity". They got it from their mama and whoever. They were both partial to machinery. Wasn't nothing they couldn't fix, and fixing took them to inventing. Built themselves an improved seed drill. Rigged a workshop upstairs in the barn. Spent nights there after chores, hammering and forging, after Moses was in his cot. Nobody knew what they were up to. Folks saw them in Oakridge looking for steel pipes and bearings. They ordered a lathe but nobody asked them what they were turning in that starless winter. You'd have seen their lamps flickering in the window that looked down on the yard. If you were going past Gilgall you coulda made out their shadows flitting like moths against the light. Musta been at least two mechanics came to see their mama before they showed up.

'To be fair to Gretta, she was never mean to the boys. I kept an eye on that. But she was distracted by bringing comfort to the menfolk, which was more than a full-time job. Maybe it showed something in the character of these lost Christians. She was neglectful of her kids in a showy way. Trigged them out classy but foolish looking with cows' licks till they were old enough to rear up. Then they grew their hairs long as they liked, smoked pipes and talked in corners amongst themselves. She lost her way with them. Let them to go wild, with no more tending than a hickory bush. To be honest, she wasn't mothering material.

'Esau and Samson didn't seem to hold nothing against her for a long while. Then, one day, I met Esau in the town. Told me he'd come in on his daddy trying to wash himself. Ribs piercing his bare pelt like he was starved. "You coulda played a tune on his chest if you'd a had a hammer," he said.

'He was right. I gave Moses a physical. Wasn't no point in pouring more dollars down his throat. Every last wore-out organ was working overtime. It just didn't seem right.

'Then two things happened. I hope this is making sense. I never spoke into no damned microphone before.

'First Moses gets himself a stroke good and proper. It pins him when he's trying to worm a bunch of calves. Fool thing to do. They couldn't get him to lift his arms. Mouth twisted. A stream of bubbles. Drool dribbling. Face greyer than a rat. Mebbie I shouldn't have, but I told him he's pooped, so he just sits rocking on the porch, following the sun with narrow eyes, letting the days slide by real slow. Gives up striving.

Samson bathes him. Esau feeds him. If he isn't in full charge of his bowels, they clean him down. Doesn't make no difference that their hearts aren't pumping his blood. Moses got no life left in him. The boys are running things and Gretta doesn't pay him no more heed than ever. It was a hard thing to see.

'Second thing, Gretta gets herself a "steady". It wasn't no mature man, no the fella she takes up with isn't no more than half her age. She was one helluva woman for fifty. And he was… an Armstrong.

'Esau and Samson told me they couldn't take it. Bad enough to have their mama on heat all the time, but Luke Armstrong – that was too big a lump of gristle to swallow.

'See, Luke figured he was a cowboy. Mighty proud of the scar on his face where an Injun had jumped him. Let on he'd killed the Injun. He woulda been better avoiding knives. Didn't have no grip on his reins. Couldn't herd cattle no more than hisself. Got them nervous and jumpy. The quietest horse woulda give up feeding for a week to get kicking him. Spent his time losing money playing at gambling and buying gin for Gretta, though I didn't begrudge her the booze. I liked a drink myself.

'The boys took it sore. Linking up with an Armstrong was holding hands with Satan. Luke was the spoiledest son of a bitch of them ever to hatch out. Cocky and smart, with a liking for bright neckties. Rode a slick horse. Made out he'd spent time learning outa books – might have impressed a stranger for a full minute and a half. Maybe it helped him talk clever to Gretta. Couldn'ta kept hisself in chewing tobacco for a day but it looked like he sure did something for her. She had a lotta needs.

'I don't know how you were brought up. The folks in Oakridge were born with quick-judging natures. But they'd seen Luke and Gretta so many times together that nobody remarked on it no more than they were asking about Moses swaying senseless in his chair. Nothing of consequence happened till Esau and Samson took it head on. Hard to say exactly what tipped them over. A thing can go on so long. Maybe they were like a water barrel filling. I don't know. Could have been they had themselves a plan from way back.

'They warned Armstrong to stay away. Told me they didn't lay hands on him then. Just took him to a corner in Casino Blanco one hot afternoon. Spoke real persuasive. Let him know he was making a fool outa their pa.

'But it made no difference to Luke and Gretta. Next time the boys went into more detail about exactly how much of Luke's member they would cut off.

'I remember telling them to walk soft. I met with Gretta, too. She looked at me the way she did. Hell, I was melting. Said she'd never been happier. Things were getting better all the time. But I saw a sadness in her. Said she was gonna have a helluva future without Moses. She told me he didn't know her no more.

'"I swear I feel like a young woman, Elias," she said, "I gotta get me a new start, or I declare, my mind's gonna rust up for good and ever." I didn't know about her mind but she was keeping her body lubricated. I didn't say what I was thinking. I thought it kinda coarse.

'They're gonna change the tape now, so don't go away.'

What was I to think? I, who had never ever read a secular book outside school. Had never frequented a picture palace, but now I'd been to Sodom. And yet, I had to be honest, I had sat and soaked up every word the doctor spoke. This was how my folks, or some of them, had turned out. Oakridge was full of Armstrongs according to Maybelle. Moses was a biblical name. Samson was the strong man in the Book of Kings. Esau had been cheated out of his blessing. Michael was the archangel and Doctor Luke wrote the third gospel but there was no sign of God in this tale as far as I could see and I wondered where He'd gone. Maybe there would be redemption in the end. I'd have to talk about that to Maybelle after side two.

Side Two

'I've been to the washroom and had a smoke and now I feel a whole lot better,' said the doc. 'Well, as I was saying, there wasn't a bigger loser than Luke Armstrong. He wasn't any better at listening than anything else he tried. Early one morning the boys find him sneaking outa the house to his horse. Tomcattin the very same as usual. He'd messed up his timing by more than a mile. Esau and Samson had been nursing a sick heifer. They were just making for their bunks when they caught him. Said they trussed him like a turkey, only a turkey woulda made less noise. Samson took a horse whip to him. Nobody enjoys being whipped. But the boys said he was squealing worse than a cartload of hogs. Wasn't easy hearing the story with guilt knocking at my own door.

'Folks said the whipping was maybe a little heavy-handed, but every lash they gave Armstrong was on account of what their mama had been doing to them their whole lives. That was an opinion. Maybe something tore loose in their heads. I've seen that kinda thing.

'When they threw Armstrong over his thoroughbred and slapped its rump to make it gallop, they must have known what was coming. But it hadn't stopped them.

'They didn't have long to sit about. By two thirty, all the Armstrongs was seen mounting up for Gilgall. They pulled a wagon that had curls of wood smoke coming out a chimney inside. Turned out to be a stove all fired up. Esau and Samson said later, they were watching from the high window of their workshop. The Armstrongs' horses stood. The Armstrong boys hung loose like gunslingers, rifles bristling outa them. Must have been some clatter of hooves. Seemed the dust hovered over their heads like a swarm. Woulda been worth seeing. Nobody knew where Gretta was.

'The boys brought Moses in off of the porch, and shuttered the windows. The Armstrongs stayed on their horses. More than likely, Luke was licking his sores under some dirty scrap of blanket. The

Armstrongs lined up in front Moses' bare pine door, rifles cocked. Then a couple of them get off of the wagon and pull long irons out of the stove. Big Marvin Armstrong roars through a bull horn, "Esau and Samson, come out now and take what you got comin, branding's gonna be way too gentle. You ain't gonna get nothing more'n you're givin your miserable, broke down bunch a steers. When we're done, we're gonna torch the whole damned place with whoever's inside. So, you're gonna smell roastin flesh. It'll be like Thanksgiving early. You'll remember this here hog roast for a long time. And Moses'll appreciate it even better because he's the hog that's gonna get cooked."

'Can't say if any of the Armstrongs picked up on the ripple of a curtain in the workshop window or heard the flicker click of the safety catches or saw Moses' boys closing one eye.

'Esau and Samson said they squinted down the sights of the two machine guns they'd been making with all that ironmongery. They were well-positioned at a height, with the Armstrongs plum in their field of vision. Then they squeezed the triggers and sent the chambers spinning and whirring and flying; they ripped up the Armstrongs, cutting them down like grass.

'"The guns were a pure delight, Doc," they told me. "Worked sweet as hell. Wasn't either of them came close to jamming."

'It was slaughter at Oakridge. Busiest time ever for the carpenters, rubbing their hands, hammering and screwing at coffins steady round the clock. Jake White dug the graves himself. Had to buy a new set of shovels on account of wear and tear. Nine funerals in a couple of days. Story made the State papers. "Final round up," they called it. A helluva lot of Armstrongs bagged in one sweep. There was a big party in Casino Blanco. Even Sheriff Hayes went. People appreciated what they'd done. But I was fretting, because Gretta had gone to ground.

'Sure, the boys got locked up for a while. They paid a couple of neighbour girls to keep an eye on Moses. Set free on appeal, seeing the Armstrongs were fixing to incinerate Moses and all. The judge was friendly. Hadn't the desire to keep them behind bars. He hated the Armstrongs.

'Moses' boys that weren't his boys, used their knowhow. Built themselves into armament production. Gave up poor farming for a good income. They said that making killing machines beat trying to keep livestock living at Gilgall. A lot of babies born around then were give the names Esau or Samson.

'Something was going on with Gretta. A while after Luke's whipping, she was seen in Oakridge viewing a consignment of embroidered hats just arrived in Miss Ida's Emporium. Ida taught Sunday School. Kept the old habits going with a few kids. She didn't approve of no immorality, but who was she to be condemning a customer with a mind to throw her green backs. At the point of selling, she found no call to think about right or wrong. She said later, that Gretta was mighty perky for a woman with a lover covered in stripes. She bought a heap of petticoats. Told Ida she wouldn't be around for a while, because she was fixing to mix with quality. Wanted to look her best. Ida said she was jumping, she was that fired up.

'Next thing Widow Lindsay's passing the dock and sees Gretta boarding *The Confederate*. Gretta's on the arm of Larry Trug, a card shark that made a monkey out of Luke late one night on the water. Worked the steamers. Was a genuine gambler. Made Armstrong look like he was sucking a comforter.

'Gretta never came back. She musta been soaking Luke right up to the point of him begging for mercy. He lost his mind big style and took up drinking full time. Passed away with cirrhosis before he was twenty-nine. I conducted the autopsy. You should have seen his liver.

'Damnedest thing of all was, after things died down, Moses made a small recovery. Still couldn't do nothing for himself, but his mind settled like the wind had stopped blowing. Was as if he'd forgot his whole troubled life, and gained some peace.

'Nobody in Oakridge, except me, ever heard from Gretta. She went the way she'd come. Like a vision that had never been. She stopped in a town called Wilson. Was soon running her own saloon. Said I should come and see her sometime.

'Not so long after, Moses died in his own bed smiling at some dream he was having. I was glad about that. After a while, Esau and Samson were lounging about in white suits with long cigars. "A country can't have too many guns," they said. Sometimes when we had a drink, the three of us together, I wondered who their real papas were. I wondered too, what they know about me and their mama, but they never said.

'I'm an old man now. I can't do much more harm. But what I find is this, so maybe you can listen up. Most people have a lot on their minds, but you never get to know what's in them. Minds are like rooms within rooms. Even when you get to the middle, you're still not there. Life isn't run to some neat formula. There's no saying what a man or a woman will do if they're treated bad enough. There's a big difference between what folks call bad morals and pure badness.

'The whole story still rattles around my head, but, as I say, it was different times. That's what I tell myself. Maybe you're a visitor in Oakridge. If you are, I hope you find what you're looking for. Living there was certainly an experience. I left in forty-nine. I guess it's changed a lot, but no matter. What I say, is that the nature of people doesn't change, no matter where you go. But sometimes, I guess, a place can take a bunch of folks and do strange things to them; that there's no accounting for it. That's all I've got to say right now. Amen.'

Oakridge had reached out and embraced me with all its depravity and despite the wickedness, I found myself smiling at Maybelle, whom I was sure must be a good woman.

'What do you reckon?' she asked. 'How much of that story are you aiming to report on?'

The words wouldn't come, at first.

'Would you like a cigarette?' she asked. 'I promise not to tell.'

I'd never smoked before.

'Those Armstrongs must have been my kin,' I said.

'Well, yes, maybe far out,' she said, pouring the coffee. 'But I wouldn't get too uptight. Our Lord himself was descended from some pretty violent men on his natural daddy's side, according to the good book. Have a cookie for the sugar hit.'

I don't know how long we must have sat there in her library. 'Why do you suppose they lost the Lord?' I asked, at last.

'I'm not a religious woman, Mr Armstrong,' she said, 'not any longer, but what I think is this: a lot of people are leaning on ranch fences, maybe for a long while, and everything looks fine. But over time the fence perishes. That's life. They go on leaning, but it's not on the everlasting arms. They're leaning on nothing. It doesn't hit them. Then one day they're asking, "What fence? I don't see no fence." I believe it must have been like that for them. It could even be they weren't ever leaning, they just thought they were. When they arrived in Oakridge, after all their travels, I guess they were full of church, but branding steers, land grabbing, dust storms and cheating stole up on them, and in the end, when they looked around them, even the postholes in the dirt had disappeared. That could have left them asking if there had ever been anything there in the first place.'

As she talked, I was thinking about my own faith, I can tell you. What was I leaning on? 'What am I going to tell the elders in Ballyrammer?' I said. 'They're all good, solid people.'

'You could tell them about fear and pity,' she said. 'Share with them the story of Moses and his patience, his forgiving nature. Let them know that those boys stood by him, no matter he wasn't their daddy. Ask them to consider how they might have done, if it had been them in Oakridge, and what they're leaning on now? You might get them to check their fences.'

'What about Gretta?' I said.

'I believe you've fallen for her too,' she said. 'Remember, her daddy was supposed to have hung himself. We don't know the ins and outs. She was a woman with a history not of her making. Ask them to figure who amongst them would have flung the first rock.'

'It's hard to believe,' I said, 'that a whole tribe could become a lost tribe.'

'Maybe, with all due respect, you're asking the wrong question,' she said. 'Could be what they brought to Oakridge was not the Lord at all, but some degraded idea of the Lord. Then when thorns and weeds sprouted, like in the story, the idea shrivelled in the sun, just like the seedlings that Jesus talked of, and they saw, if they looked at all, that their notion of God was so much baloney. Who's to say it wouldn't have happened to you, or me. Except, I don't hold with all that now.'

'Is that what you think?' I kept repeating. 'Should I tell them that?'

'I'm for honesty,' she said, 'but it's your call. If you've got to tell them something, that might be as close as you're going to get.'

I was right about Maybelle. She was an honourable woman. 'How long have you got?' she said. 'I've a heap more tales of Oakridge, if you're interested. And the Doc's got all day.'

I told her I'd hear them all.

But that night I didn't sleep. I lay in my American room, under the tinny rotations of the ceiling fan and wondered if I should listen to the other tapes. As the stifling night hours ground away, a rooster began to crow. I felt lonely and disturbed in that cheap motel, as if I'd stared into some brackish pool and seen a reflection I couldn't quite make out, and heard the echo of my own words returning to me, distorted, void, and unanswered.

Still Life

Somewhere, back then, within the cave of Louis's café, an accordionist plays in the French style, but they're on a loop. Old-fashioned music. Tremulous. Soulful. Don't get me wrong, I love that stuff, but I'm a lone spirit and I get maudlin in the early hours. Mostly I feel vulnerable. It's hard to trust anyone, so I carry a weapon.

People outside are talking Watergate. But who cares? To me it's nothing. I'm on Death Wish Coffees at my usual table. It's oval, with a bluish mock-marble top. Warmer to touch than the real thing because it's plastic, like the seats. There are maybe eight tables. I'm giving you the lowdown. There's a jukebox, freestanding, with Streisand and Terry Jacks inside – maybe you remember his song about leukaemia. It's high on purple neon, but it doesn't play. I'm not knocking it, though. It's company.

So, there's me, and this youngish couple. That's all. They're together and not together. You know how it is late on, and the young man is staring at Louis' mural. I know it well and love it. It's of a beautiful woman.

'Is there a stark beauty in lonely people, do you think?' This is the question the young woman asks the young man, in a kind of whisper.

He's one of those dark-slick hair types in a square-shouldered jacket. A carnation in his lapel. His necktie's broad and striped, diagonal. You know what I mean? Burnt tangerine, with chevrons, off centre. Would I buy a jalopy from him if I had the dough? Are you kidding me? In his handshake hand, he grips a plain red mug of coffee. Just holds it, like he's going to drink it in slow motion. Like in a cinema. But he doesn't drink. He's a poser. An actor. Reminds me of a picture I saw of a fella in Pompeii that the ash fell on. Like he got stuck in time.

Louis has dimmed the lights a little, out of kindness. Thirteen shell orbs stretch into the cave. But he keeps a spot on the mural. Through wooden window slats, old sister moon ribs one side of the young man's face, lending him a deathly, striped pallor. The pinkie on his left hand is missing. His shirt is corpse-pale too. His cuffs are on display.

On the angular table before him, lies one of Louis' standard plates and on the plate, like a flattened cadaver, an uneaten slice of pecan pie. His fork appears unused. The young man's mind is… on the mural. At first, I don't object.

'Get real, kid,' he tells his girlfriend. He calls her 'Flooz'.

I guess you'd say she was a looker. Big heavy bloom of hair. Filling one of those luminous, translucent blouses, of some see-through material to show off her curves. From what I can see, her skin has that ripe, come-and-peel-me look favoured by men and the creators of fleshy artwork. But she has soft eyes. She holds her mouth open a little, the way he likes, high cheekbones fragile, eyes fixed on her lover looking at the mural. Her left hand rests close to, but not within a mile of his. I'm getting it. Oh, and she wears a fake gold, square-dial watch. I remember it was 4:05 am and they were still pretty juiced up.

So, what was with the mural? I called her Amorette because she had to be French. She sits at her own table but I count her a pretty close affiliate. No, more than that, I come and talk with her after the clubs. In the vacuum, after the music stops. Louis never shuts. He keeps a bottle of Bourbon for his regular nightjars. Me and Amorette are… close. Loners, but a twosome. Over time I've told her stuff. Got to know her slowly. Best way. Personal things.

But now this jerk is beginning to bug me. He keeps gazing at her on the wall, like she's some sort of object. I'm feeling more than a little tense. His woman watches him staring at my girl. It's been a tough week. A long night. I'm wanting to talk to her, you know, on my own. I have health issues and I'm in a bad place. He isn't serious about his love life or his coffee. I'm not keen on the way he's looking at Amorette.

A sudden flicker. A flash of fire. He lights a Lucky, and from his well-formed lips, a snake-thin stream of smoke.

Amorette ignores him. She's seen it all. She looks down at me, in her cream cloche hat that dips on her pedigree head, at just the most perfect angle, a model in her elegant green coat that's trimmed with fur. That's what attracted me to her. That, and a whole lot more. Take for instance her right hand. Bare. Always bare, I tell you. Her delicate fingers grasp the china handle of her cup. She often reads my leaves. She's got class, that's what I'm trying to say. And I love her mind. She's no ordinary woman.

What if a few sparrow-crumbs fall on her lap? Okay, she's a real person. She lives and breathes. I pick them off, if my hand's not shaking, but there's no hanky-panky. I respect her too much. Just beyond where she sits, a pile of waxy apples balances on a ledge. Life is precarious. 'Would you care for a piece of fruit?' she says. So damned polite. I say, 'Naw, but thanks for the offer.'

Let's say we're intimate. We've talked about love and death. She'd come from Paris, God knows how many years before. What the hell for, I'll never know. She'd worked in a gallery near the Seine. Knew all the main painters but she didn't have to tell me. I could tell. She has exquisite legs, but I don't look at them. I'm not some sort of pervert, and there's more to life than lust. I love her in my heart. She's my Amorette.

So, the jerk starts getting fresh. Not with his own woman but with mine. There's no sign of Louis. It's not a real automat, but sometimes he goes out for a while and kinda leaves me in charge. Nothing formal.

'That broad can dress,' says the young man to his companion. She shrugs. Why should she care about some fresco in an all-night café?

I'm loaded but I don't like where he's going. She's drumming her fingers on their table, like she wants to leave but she doesn't dare. She shivers, as you do in the dawn.

'Why can't you dress like her?' he says.

I'm thinking, Bastard.

But morons like him can read your mind. He's getting the vibes. Wants me to agree. Knows what I'm thinking. Okay, we're entombed in Louis's, as the stars fade, in a cavern in Hell's Kitchen. There's him and his woman, me and Amorette.

He's in my face. 'You got something to say, dork, huh?' his voice is rising. His woman's saying, 'No,' but he's coming at me out of the drink. This has got to be a dream.

'What you think of this snazzy bitch on the goddamn wall?' he says.

I'm saying nothing but he's not taking it.

'I've been watching you, freak,' he says, 'you want to screw her too?'

I'm still not speaking.

'I'll tell you what she thinks of you, pig face,' he says, 'I'll show you.' He takes the red mug of coffee, thick as molasses and throws it in her face. On Amorette. It's like spitting on an icon. I watch it fly, slowly, like in a movie. There's a dull whump as the mug cracks defenceless, white delft showing inside its skin. It's mud splashing her face, oozing in gobs off her creamy bell hat, over the moss-green coat. It's defilement. He turns to his girl. 'Underneath she's a common whore like you,' he says, then he hits her hard about the body, like a fighter.

His woman screams. He pulls a knife to cut her. She's begging him.

I bring out the weapon. It's ready to go. I'm smelling execution, but I shoot him in the leg. One bullet for his woman, and three for Amorette.

Louis appears. Calls 911… The woman whimpers. She's holding his head. I'm frozen. I never shot a man before. Louis is on the ball with his mop and bucket, slopping the floor. The cops have me in cuffs.

Louis painted her out. 'I tried to clean her up,' he wrote me, 'waste of time. Her colours ran. She was a mess. I got a guy to remove her. You got any ideas for a new picture?'

The young man got probation. Very big deal. His young woman got a ruptured spleen. Still scared, she wouldn't talk. I got ten years and a lot of shocks for being a violent psychotic with alcohol.

I didn't reply to Louis, but after they let me out, I paid him a visit one pleasant May afternoon. Things change. He looked older. I'd stopped drinking. At first, he didn't know me. I didn't know the place. Total makeover. Bright lime and yellow. A lemonade parlour. He fixed me an ice cream soda on the house. And a Nescafe.

In daylight, the space felt different. Bigger and wider. More air and windows. Time at work. No trace of her. Her wall was white and blank. Like snow.

'So, you didn't replace her?' I said, sitting on an aluminum mushroom.

'I changed my mind,' he said, 'out of courtesy.'

'To her?' I said.

'To you both,' he said, raising a glass. I always had time for Louis.

'Where do people go when you paint them out?' I asked. 'Just wondering.'

'Now there's a question,' he said, 'but hey, nobody's painted you out, buddy. You're looking good. You've gained a little weight, wherever you've been. Damned sure you have. And it suits you. Want a refill?'

'Okay,' I said. 'Why not?'

Inspired by Edward Hopper (1882–1967), 'Automat' and a shot from 'Twin Peaks'.

Night Jarred in Colette's

It was my last night. I'd seen them before in 'Colette's', the two girls at the next table who had to be sisters – maybe twins, though they weren't dressed the same, and they didn't talk like sisters. What age were they underneath? Perhaps late twenties? Maybe a whole lot more, below the pallid make believe. In front of them stood one of the usual glass decanters, for anyone wanting to dilute. In my experience, over two weeks, no one did. Why would they water down anaesthesia? I actually wondered why she bothered. Colette, I mean. Setting them out. I guessed it was for entirety, and the love of art.

It had been that sort of trip. The Seine, street artists, *bateaux mouches*. But it had lacked something until I found Colette's.

Outside was a crushing life of sorts. But inside her *taverne*, she had created something better. Something of faux authenticity, and all absorbing, with retro gaslight that spat, and spittoons for modern gentlemen, who didn't. A nice touch. 'Spittoon' is one of those comical period words. I rhymed it with '*Puckoon*'. There were, inevitably, a host of bevelled mirrors. One found oneself retreating behind the surface, infinitely multiplied in diminishing sizes. There was no beer. Not even bottled. Only corked wines and the more arcane spirits to attract a perceptive crowd. The girls, I noticed, were on absinthe. Cloudy and writerly. I looked more closely. Hard to know if they were hunting or the hunted. Probably a bit of both.

'Tonight, you are your part.' Always tonight. This was the sign that hung above Colette's long luminous bar, her strapline, as we say nowadays. 'You are what you perform.' And it was true. The performers were the audience. And vice versa. The gap had closed. Tonight was every night, if you could afford it. I couldn't, but I went every night. I felt compelled.

No one was real. 'Real, darling, is a killer,' was what she said, working the crowd, thin as a wisp, wiry as a brush dislodging debris. 'We never play ourselves. Not here. Not in Colette's.'

Mimi – I'll call her that – had possibly been gazing in my direction for a while. But probably not. I couldn't catch her looking. There was something about the way she held her mouth. Like it had been broken and reset. Her teeth appeared to have grown with rapacious intent. I remember wondering how many dead carcasses she might have stripped? But then, what was she thinking about me, dressed in my rented jacket and top hat, as one did, with my stick-on Tartuffe beard? Oh stop. What did I think about myself?

Mimi held her lips like the entrance to a cave, or a mineshaft maybe. It was a strange look to have cultivated. The tough hairs of her blonde, bleached wig were piled up at the back, but an endearing kiss curl had been teased out on her forehead, like a straying casual thought. Her green eyes arrested me – how she appeared to keep them averted like the hidden glass marbles of a boy.

She wore a handsome blue gown, which gave her an icy appearance, like water about to freeze. There was also the rouge. The imperative, round blotches on each cheek. Applied and patted like clichéd old roses. She looked reassuringly contrived. This, I felt, was her honest allure.

In fact, it wasn't easy to find the precise target of her gaze. It fell somewhere between me and infinity. I was attracted to her, I will not lie. I wanted to speak with her. To say I'm Ireland's Hemmingway or

Fitzgerald. I ached to read her a sonnet. One of my own, no doubt. But that had been the story of my life, such as it was. Aching without achieving. Still, I supposed, each vintage night lifted the curtain on a new possibility. Tomorrow, I would take my flight. How cowardly that sounded but how savagely true.

Carmel, let's say her maybe twin, was a different proposition. She had spoken to Colette in deep tobacco tones. I was afraid she would target me and penetrate my shell. In an instant, I believed that she could see right through me, like looking up some pipe and seeing the daylight, which made me tremble.

She wore black fur. A trophy perhaps. Her head attire – the most stygian shade of purple – was a sort of crenelated flowerpot with some small rodent resting on the crown – a mouse, or bat – to shock, though hopefully made of felt. The coat might have been her grandmother's. The sharpness of her features was shrouded by a veil. Thin and sheer with beauty spots, but delicate so that one could admire her through it, as if she were an iced cake in the window of a patisserie. Her orange lips shone waxy like those of a Tussaud model. I liked her peeping coral ears especially, white and scalloped as they were, and exactly in proportion. Her doll's face swivelled this way and that as she followed the evening forensically, noting its ups and downs, its little, abortive, diverting coups and dramas. Her dainty hands remained at rest – except when she reached for her liquor glass or lighted another Disque Bleu.

Not to smoke was not to live.

For four hours every night, I had made Colette's my home, after flirting with the galleries and boulevards. There, I had found my stage, where I lived life gloriously, though briefly, as time ran out.

And around me, how the people talked. A bulbous woman, using obscene language wore a slash in the back of her dress, and a kind of coronet woven through her hair. She spoke of Cubists. Two square-faced men with diamond piggy eyes puffed fat cigars and wheezed out laughter.

Alone, I threw myself into Colette's. It was really so absorbing.

A long-haired wannabe, whose appearance may have strongly resembled that of Oscar at the beginning of his odyssey, strummed a tortured instrument. Love sickness on show. The more demonstrative patrons dropped francs – which one could buy for euros – from an ostentatious height – into his flat green poisonous dish. Clink, clink, metal on china. Until the china cracked or he had enough to drink.

Someone in a waistcoat read Camus in a corner, in a German accent, which sounded odd. As the night advanced, I was being swallowed one last time. Who would tomorrow belong to? Ah well, I'd see.

Colette had – how would I describe it – a little balcony within her palace. High up in a gable, accessed by some secret steps no doubt, and protruding eerily from the wall, like a swallow's nest.

At midnight a violinist appeared, bowing tragically. A wraith, a woman probably, though it was hard to tell. By now, later trysts had largely been arranged. And happy assignations made, so that the spectral keening was simply ironic. At the end of the piece, Colette, now in a red sheath dress, raised an arm in casual salute, with studied carelessness, as if it had all been a surprise, and said, '*Mon Dieu, quelle performance.*'

I cheered with the rest.

Then, as a reward to the crowd, her aproned boys brought finger food. Timeless round dots of paté, and oysters, which I believe they used to do in Dublin.

Always and forever, the crowd sang loud-stamping, ribald songs. Some stood on Colette's rickety tables to bawl, so acute was their emotion, others removed their clothing as another evening climaxed in totality.

At this point, I pretended to consult the antique pocket watch, which had come with the jacket, glancing about me in case someone should want my attention.

Colette called us 'friends'.

Night following night I had drunk too much, saturating my empty capillaries with the delicious warmth of strangers, the comfort of unknown pulses, assuring myself that a drowning anonymity was what I needed. This night had been no exception. But in my heart, I wondered what it would be like to go home with someone, to smell their wax melt in some back street *mansarde*. With Mimi perhaps, teeth or no teeth, or with the convincing verminous Carmel, or even, God save me, with Colette herself. Such are the musings of the mad and mesmerised.

Could I please a woman? Make her purr? I had always been a hackneyed island. Surely in that construction there was an art. I had made my way tortuously, treading life's mottled paths like a stranger, searching, always searching. Like I didn't belong. But here in the immensity of Colette's, I at least felt at one. A part of where I was meant to be.

Perhaps tonight?

The girls did not acknowledge me, though, before they left. Perhaps below the paint, they were arid civil servants, or museum curators? Their gear was all top drawer.

But speculation, as someone must have said, is idle. The night was upending like a chamber pot. I was draining the dregs. At first, there was the usual commotion of separation, the sloppy intimate promises and nicotine kisses, then the shadow people slid away as they always did, shallowly limping into nothingness. Souls, if we have souls, simply dissolved, dripping like Dali's clocks, viscous ghosts reclaiming the space and energy for the next time.

I watched as Colette and her team went to work. Wet-wiping, emptying ashtrays with rapid functional movements, brutally straightening the bentwood chairs, dustpanning debris, sweeping, sweeping the night away and leaving it, *parfait*.

That final time, I sat on, thinking of what might lie ahead in the pretend cosmos I normally inhabited. How could I go back? What was left at the end of such evenings, if it wasn't the conscious absence of presence? The acid almostness of a photographic negative. Had the breaths, so recently mingled, in any sense, continued? Could I bottle them and take them with me?

'Really, it's time, *mon cher*,' Colette told me, hovering robotically, like a crimson arachnoid, without compassion. 'Come back sometime again and see me. Until then...' She blew me a brittle kiss. 'Every night we have unreality in Colette's, you know.'

I didn't move.

'It is all here for you,' she said, with menace, 'every time.'

My body froze as her boys closed in.

I dithered.

'*Monsieur*,' she said, flicking a modern rejection switch. The room lit up. Light blazed electrically. It looked much smaller. Narrower. Improbably stark and shabby. I shielded my eyes, fearing for my retinas. We cannot bear too much.

'I told you, *mon chéri*,' she said, pointing to the door with one jagged finger. 'The show... is over.'

'Good night.' I said.

'*La fin, monsieur*,' she said. '*Toujours la fin.*'

Inspired by Louis Anquetin (1861–1932), 'Bar Scene', c. 1891.

Dark Secret

I'm sure you know that letting a house for money can be an awful burden as well as an advantage. That's what they don't tell you. But for all that, I'll give you a story about the luck I had myself a while ago.

It all started before I was conceived at all, when a bit of solder jumped out of a water pipe above the ceiling in the 'in-between' below the floor above. This left exposed the nail-hole made by some clown of a workman around the time of *Titanic*. Instead of him cutting out a tidy section and joining the two ends with a grand piece of strong copper, like a decent plumber, didn't he do the wicked thing and slap on an oul sticking plaster and say to himself that it would do rightly.

Well, you might as soon have jammed in a mouthful of Beech-Nut chewing gum for all the good it did when it was put under pressure. And in life it's the pressure that counts.

But tell me this, wasn't the back boiler the quare invention? What? Weren't the half of us reared with our buckets of weekend bathwater heated by shiny black British coal brought in on boats, and it roaring away pleasantly for all that in the iron grate, and grand music when you heard the gurgling inside the wall.

But weren't we the wise ones then to take no chances with the like of an explosion behind the fire when we spent our time racing up the stairs and opening the big broad taps in the deep bath and letting it gush like your man in Yellowstone Park, all steaming and fierce like it was boiling from the middle of the earth?

The young ones nowadays has no practical sense, for all their book learning. They don't know the workings of the pipes beyond the flames and didn't the two lassies that I rented me cottage to for next to nothing, stoke the fire with the generous mountain of turf I was foolish enough to leave them, and forget entirely to turn on the pump.

And then, to take the biscuit, if they didn't go out for a vindaloo fit to strip the skin off their mouths and a video, leaving the whole place to itself without a soul for supervision. And when they came in, with Hugh Grant and the rest of it, wasn't water coursing down the walls like Niagara and it trailing the plasterboard with it, the way it took all the enjoyment out of the film and spoiled altogether their relish for poppadoms.

Didn't I know rightly they had been flirting with the lad that takes the orders in the 'Mumbai Tiger' and laughing and making eyes at him, and lolling around the film shop looking for boys, and during all that, a spout of vapour was blowing my pipe to hell.

I can tell you they were soon on the phone, crying and telling me all about it.

'Oh help,' they said, 'you must come quickly; a shocking thing is taking place in your house, at this very moment.'

I was not happy to see my ceiling lying dead on the floor, in a sort of whitened mush. All the same, I did the Christian thing, and resolved in my heart not to be cross on account of them being from other lands and because of their young ages and lovely smiles and the great manners their mammies had taught them, so out of politeness I said I'd have it as good as new in no time at all.

The divil of it was that one of them had climbed on a collapsible stool to investigate the torrents by poking her head into the hole above and hadn't she slipped in an awkward way and ended up with a right shiner of a black eye and wasn't I palpitating for fear of a claim.

Well, it never rains but it pours and before I knew, I was plunged into another intriguing mystery. The first signs of the new puzzle appeared in the door jamb of my kitchen, opposite the fan oven a rascal of a salesman had persuaded me to buy, and it was as like a mushroom as ever you seen, squeezing persistently through a crack in the wood in a bold, pushy way and looking very impertinent.

I have always been partial to the cooked breakfast, especially the back bacon and Clonakilty with an egg, and I was thinking of slicing it off and throwing it on the pan with a whack of lard, when I remembered the ones in England that paralysed themselves for months from eating red, white-spotted toadstools. So, I sprayed it with stuff out of a bottle from McMahons that was supposed to be lethal and for all that, it wasn't a bit of use.

But be warned, if ever you're tempted to involve the government with a mushroom problem don't bother yourself, for I got one of them soft-faced fellas out of the council, with a clipboard in his hand and nothing in his head and he pretended to study the mushroom. Oh yes, he must have walked past it a dozen times, like he was putting a spell on it, then he told me he had never seen the like of it and when I asked him about spores making you choke – for I had been reading up about them – he looked at me very alarmed and blew his nose in a big hanky and said I should open the windows immediately, for he was convinced that galloping condensation lay at the root of the whole conundrum.

Then, suddenly he told me he was in a great hurry for he had a dozen more deadly cases to visit, though he hoped mushrooms would not be among them. He told me not to fret, for he would be writing a long report and he was the very boy for it, what with the list of letters the length of a donkey's tail after his name and a substantial mileage allowance, it was sure to turn out well. 'Though it may take a while,' he said. Then he folded himself, like an ironing board, into the low car he came in, and said he was never off the road, burning up rubber for the good of humanity, and working for the authorities.

The girls were sleeping on couches in a house of hormonal lads and I was worried for their morals. So, I changed the tactics right away and answered an advert for 'Tidy Workers and Damp Investigators' in the local paper that would tackle all the problems together, and I was only delighted by the rapid response I got, and in no time I had a robust team of fine men in yellow jackets, every one of them holding a hammer and an opinion. And they were talking together and smoking and taking off their hats and scratching their heads with their fingernails and saying, 'Ho ho,' and was there any tea going, in a very professional way.

Before I knew, they were tearing into the place like termites and pulling up floorboards and what did they find if it wasn't a field of mushrooms underneath, growing splendidly, like long spindly legends in the darkness and them spreading like ropes across the joists below, like they were working for the boy with the horns.

Well, the banging they were making and the terrible exclamations coming out of their mouths and the *boys a boys* and *the like o' that*s, was so loud I clapped my hands over my ears for the sake of sanity. Then the head man spits on his calloused hands and says with excitement, 'Bring in them tools and the big drum.'

'Easy on,' says I, there is no call for party tunes, for the natives here only fights once a year. But it turned out to be a plastic container with some class of deadly chemical in it for exterminating mushrooms that would offend nobody. It took three of them to carry it, for it was a fair weight and full of gallons.

They were spraying a fine mizzle for days without masks. I could see that they were hard men and it didn't affect them, although they spluttered like patients in a sanatorium. They said they were used to it and that they had, every one of them, great pairs of lungs, on account of the strong tobacco they smoked and the bawdy songs they sang in confined spaces.

I was well pleased with them for they were a noble squad of mechanics altogether and to be fair, they only used the F-word when they ran out of cigarettes.

They were near to finishing the entire removal of my kitchen floor and still on the trail of the fungus when they came across a suspicious bunch of rocks that they needed to prise up and four of them were swinging on the end of the crowbar. They all heaved at the same split second, saying, 'One, two, three,' and when they gave it the big one, didn't we all hear a mighty gurgle and a splash and standing there with our mouths open didn't we only watch till the hole they were in filled with a black liquid, the thickness of treacle. In no time they were in the middle of an oozing pool in their strong boots with the steel toes, and letting it lap over their feet.

I thought, at first, that it was Guinness, which would have been ideal. But I wanted to be sure. 'What is it at all?' says I, acting the innocent, and shaking at the edge of the pond. All the same, I was thinking of sending for the clergy the way I was scared, for I've a fear of miracles and things beyond. Then the foreman dips his finger into it and raises it to his nose and he licks it and grins like he isn't wise and says, 'I think so,' and 'Get away,' and he asks for milk bottles and jam pots and empty honey jars and a baking bowl that was holding a plant. And weren't the fellas filling them up and whispering and holding them up to the light and closing the yard door at the back to keep out the chickens and other nosey characters. And wasn't I standing there looking into the hole and it filling again as quick as they emptied it and thinking to myself, what under God was going on at all.

Then the gaffer takes off his white helmet and clears the throat, and says he to me, 'We've struck oil.'

'Ha, ha,' says I, and he starts talking about gift horses and seams in the ground and cracks and subterranean pockets and shales and drills, till me head is splitting.

'I swear to God, you've an oil well in yer kitchen, mister,' he says. So I sat down for it was hard to take in.

'Is there men in the council that does oil wells?' says I. 'For I could see it would be a damnable nuisance walking round it with pots of spuds, and I had a fair idea the two girls wouldn't be used to the like of that at all and they might leave me forever.

Well, if they didn't all begin to laugh and slap their legs and push each other about and say, 'Did you hear that?' and 'Well, well,' and 'Jiminy be.'

The foreman says to me there was hefty deposits below and we were going to be rich and I wasn't keen on the way he used the word, 'we'. I thought he was putting me in the way of temptation like Adam in the garden and I was getting ready to say no to whatever he suggested, for I thought, after all, he was a man with an air of presumption. But then he asked me did I know about valves and stopcocks and barrels and pipes and before I knew, hadn't I signed a contract with him on the back of an electric bill for wouldn't they have squealed like pigs to the Revenue if I hadn't agreed.

I had to tell a half-lie to the girls, God forgive me, and them going on for teachers of children, that the mushrooms were poisonous and it could take years before the cottage would be fumigated and they were not slow to agree that their studies were sure to be long over by then.

I was sad to see them go, for in every other way they had been a joy, but I bade them farewell and forgave them for allowing me house to blow up. I was never the man to hold a grudge.

Well, didn't I meet them anyway in 'Sandino's' one heavy Saturday night, playing whistles and bodhráns like Galway girls, and drinking pints of porter, the best ever you seen, when I was still out celebrating my new business. And weren't they all over me, buying me drinks and showering me with powerful hugs and kisses the way they wondered why some fine strapping woman hadn't snapped me up years ago, the treasure I was, and a man of means.

My Own Front Door

28 October,
Michaelmas Mews.

Dear Volunteer,

It's hard to believe that autumn has arrived already. Phew! Thanks for your interest. I may just be the sort of client you are looking for, but of course it's up to you. I thought you might want to know a bit more about me. To clue you in. To help you decide if you want to invest time in me. So here goes.

All my stuff had been in storage since God knows when. Personal effects they call them. In a tea chest. They kept it in the basement of the main building, in the bowels below, beside the big old, glass standby batteries, which were fascinating and the emergency diesel Perkins generator. Vroom, vroom. Imagine if the lights were to blow in a loony bin! Sister Johnston took me down there once to reassure me. 'It's all waiting for you, Amber,' she said.

Hospital Orders, as I'm sure you know, are indeterminate. You will have covered this in your training. They hold you until they think you're safe to be let out. In stages. It can be slow. I worked in the walled garden for years, in rubber gloves to protect my hands, murdering no one, except the slugs. Seriously. Sometimes I baked in the rehab kitchen. It was a good programme. And here I am today.

This will be the first December to be semi on my own. Well, subject to supervision.

I'm not allowed to wander off. I gave them my word, but there's also serious CCTV. Lots of.

I'm never far from a beady Cyclops' eye. They call it 'Intensive monitoring' because they can't take any chances with me. Not with my record.

I'm planning a mini-Christmas already, with a little tree and things, but stop, I'm jumping ahead. My sheltered bungalow was built specially – as one of four – in the grounds, among the beech trees. I like to think I'm living in a park. There are certainly acres of forest and piles of fat grey squirrels, though they're infecting the red ones. Personally, I would gas them. My new home measures 675 square feet, I believe. I don't like metres. It's actually a shoebox made of bricks, not straw or wood, so that no big bad wolf will blow it down. Just let him try! It has no aesthetic quality, that I can see. I think it looks like a toilet block. But I have a kind of rent book, so technically I'm a tenant.

Don't get me wrong, I'm not knocking it. It's certainly something. There's a bedroom for me and a kind of cupboard for the stuff. Outside, I have a flower patch. With real soil.

They even granted me an overlapped wooden hut, so it's like an allotment just for me. I've been resettled well away from most people – I don't know who they put in the other three bungalows on the outer rim of normality. In the mornings, when the sun shines through a gap in the trees, it lights up my face, I'm told. So that's good.

Today I'm lifting the dahlias, which did pretty well. They say a frost is coming. Bad news. When I'm not horticulturing, as I call it, I'm working my way through the things.

Sifting, you know. It's a ruminative process. Inevitably bovine. The older I grow, the more I wonder what is buried in the ground below us, waiting for resurrection, for good or evil. If it's not the bones or souls of children, it's the spirits of their mothers, embalmed in bogs. I'd say the Earth's crust holds every human memory since the world began, every private thought (shudder, shudder) the weft and warp lodged in clay or loam. Scrub and grasses on the surface, but far below, roots tapping deep. Perhaps you don't agree?

I'll soon be forty, just so as you know. Crows' feet. Help! Not a young forty. I don't drink now. They don't permit it. It was, 'Hugely disinhibiting,' according to my medical notes, which I have read. Medication ruins libido and softens your teeth. I'm all seed heads really. You will be safe enough. No hope of love.

I'd been thinking a lot about Mum when I rediscovered her tiny diary at the bottom of the chest. Debbie asked me – she's my key worker – if I'd seen it before? I told her I didn't know. But doubtless, I lied. I'd blanked it out because that was what had finally ignited me, you know, if you will forgive the pun. Joke. Confidentiality – don't start me.

And no, I don't miss the ward. Well not the people in 'Columbanus', who are nuts, but I suppose, if I'm honest, though who is entirely honest, I feel the want of something. Routine probably, the blood tests and so on. The nurses are in and out as per my care plan but it's not the same. Not that I would go back. Press on, I say.

I'm sure you know about modern drugs. They dampen the creative spirit of impulsivity.

Serotonin and neuroreceptors. That jazz. I've borrowed books from the hospital library and read it up. It's fascinating.

Anyway, there's more to unpacking than you might imagine. I'm considering a guinea pig for company. They turned me down for the white, long-tailed guys. Say no more. People are funny about rats. But squirrels are rodents too. The authority would buy it through the Comforts Fund.

How antiquated is that? I'd have to feed it. Do you like pets?

Mum was sixteen when she was writing her log, recording it in red biro. Significant or what? She had swallowed *The Bell Jar* whole. Gulp. No doubt you know it. 'There ought, I thought, to be a ritual for being born twice – patched, retreaded and approved for the road.' Sylvia's words. Aren't they arresting? The excerpt is from page 233 of my copy.

Sylvia was so screwed up. Hughes was a super smart bastard. I'd like to be born again, so it's very apt. I was twenty-one when I crashed and did the dreadful thing. I'd never liked men.

Not the sort who preyed on Mum, or me. She was dead six months by then. There was no gas oven involved. Her ending was elemental, in water, like Virginia's.

Debbie hadn't heard of Virginia. Some days I sit in the cupboard – actually a room the size of a bread bin – like a Buddha, on the floor, and think. Such a small book, with its cramped, lined pages. So much clamped in. So much left out.

Mum drew daffodils, the way girls did back then, beside the date. Miniatures, at first quite bright, but later with tattered petals and phallic trumpets. Enough said.

Her entries grew dark and short.

Love Tess, hate Troy,

that sort of thing, inside a heart.

I'm fond of reading. I hope that you like books.

17 March, St Patrick's Day:
Mr P predicts an 'A' – he's lovely!!!

Elaborate shamrocks. That was an 'A' in English at the Grammar. Mr P was Mr Porter, I knew that much. There were smudges on the page. All this still smoulders when I'm alone in the hut, or the shed, if you prefer, when I'm shaking off dirt from corms, inhaling her memory among the riddles. I'm not a fire hazard now but I'm not allowed to smoke on my own. I'm risk assessed regularly, so, don't worry on that score. No alcohol. Sometimes I talk to her in the gloom. It's not a secret. I do hear voices, but I'm not psychotic – I've read Ron Coleman. If you haven't, look him up. I love his insight. I think he's great. I sense Mum's presence among the spades and strawberry bird nets, and it's a comfort. She did her best for me and she was a good woman.

With tubers you can take precautions. You store them dry. Clothe them in old copies of *The Times*, and if you're lucky, they'll survive. But they mightn't, you see. And that's the pity. Some do turn to mush. You can't predict which ones will perish. It's not their fault.

With life, there's no telling either. Some people survive it fine. Apparently. You wouldn't know they'd lived it. At present, I feel all right, but I think that humans are a lot like dahlias, and just as easily destroyed, don't you think?

I have always maintained, in my own head, that I did not do it. That's my position, which will not change. After my entire flat was enveloped by the flames, I said I couldn't remember. That's all I said. I said I was drunk. So was Mr Wrong. You really don't want to know. I made it. He didn't. QED. Well not quite, but I can't tell you more than that.

'Intentional,' they said, 'lethal when under the influence.' I was skin-grafting in the burns unit for ages before they sent me home. Not literally. He was well crisped. They thought that I was also dangerous with knives, but that was ruled out early. At the time I elected to be mute. I'd had no opportunity to kill Mr P, though that would have been super.

It would also have been – a nine-letter word beginning, coincidentally, with P. Which I think is interesting. I'll let you work it out. I'm fond of puzzles. Jigsaws, anything. No, P was long off the scene by then, and undoubtedly in hell, though I know where he's buried.

They asked me about my inner world. The forensic mob. My stars! I know all the questions as well as the answers. My fantasies? Eventually I began to talk. We've covered my whole life more than once. Sometimes they send students, for me to help them with their training. I'm called an 'expert patient'. I take the girls, but not the men. They know not to ask me. I've met a lot of interesting, strong, young women. They're always grateful.

Some of them send me 'thank you' cards for sharing. I'll let you see them if you decide to become my buddy. Debbie thinks I'm as sane as she is. And I say, 'Who can tell?'

'Happy days,' I say, 'we're girls together.'

They don't like labels these days, or so they tell you. So they never call me the 'A' word to my face. But I'm not stupid. My genes saw to that, on both sides, I suppose.

I enjoy growing perennials but I totally adore the big spiky dahlias, which is kind of weird.

My favourite is one that turned blood orange all by itself. Nobody would believe it had started off white. Nature or nurture? There you go.

'Ah, away with you,' said Debbie, who's lovely. Dahlias send out green shoots in spring.

Mum's entries stopped – almost. I think she lost heart.

> *6 May:*
> *Tried to revise D.H.* (That would be Lawrence.)
> *Hopeless. He's just too much.* (I read on. That wasn't Lawrence.)
> *Can't concentrate.*

That made me tremble. But it was what came next that got me.

> *1 June:*
> *God help me. P is for prick. What will I do?*

The sheer starkness of it.

Nothing more in the in-between, only the horror of it, until delivery.

24 December:
Lost pints of blood. Premature. Four pounds, one ounce.
Crome Yellow. (Borrowed no doubt from Huxley). *Jaundiced.*
A girl.

That was me. ME!

She had never told me – or anyone – who impregnated her, so he got off. Seeing his initial written down had been a shock. But it had helped explain so much. The half thoughts I'd had. It had given me the inside track. But it had flipped me. I'd often wondered where I got the urge to teach, not that it matters now. A foisted spoonful of rancid sperm was all it took to start me off in the belly of a schoolgirl.

Hard times she had, we had, the two of us. Oh, yes, we had. Though, I liked *Hard Times* by Dickens, ironically. There's a song and a sigh of the weary with the same name. The McGarrigles sang it. They are Canadians. Do you enjoy folk music? I like to sing. I also want a ukulele. Soon it will be my b'day. So, who knows? Christmas Eve in my own place. Two birthdays, very nearly, for the price of one. It's as good as it gets.

Imagine, though. My own front door. They let me pick the colour. I chose yellow, defiantly, for hope. It will be priceless though. Oxen on their knees at midnight. All that lowing! I'll roll it all into one big celebration. If you can make it, it will be incredible, though soft drinks only. Now you know why. I've invited Debbie and the team, since they are my friends – why not – to give her a poinsettia from the Green House. That's another project on the site. I think she'll like the crimson bracts. Though it's pointless keeping them. They've all been forced and once they're gone, they never come back. 'I'll dump you, boys,' I'll tell them, 'when you lose your colour.' There's anger still.

Oh, and she's bringing four cinnamon-scented candles and a walnut-cake from Marks. It was Mum's favourite. Scrummy, eh? There'll be plenty for us all. Perhaps you really will come?

Mum never came to the wards, but I'm hoping she'll call this year to see my place. I almost believe in that. I hope she does. I'll save her a slab, in any case, and leave it on a sepulchral plate, with a fork, tines down, in case of accidents, like we used to do for Santa (I want him to be a woman).

Anyway, I'm going to lie down for a while now in my secluded room with Iris Dement. I hadn't meant to go on and on. If you can't read this handwritten scrawl, tell them I'd love a laptop. It's supposed to be in the plan, but it could take a while. That's all for now. Let me know if you are a woman and, if you're interested in flowers, I'd love to meet you. I do so much want a volunteer. I think we could be friends. Real friends, you know. Honestly, I do.

Yours,
Amber

P.S. I'm giving Nicorette a go. Headway!!

The Jinx

Maybe some thinking is unchangeable and there's nothing you can do but accept it. The way it is, the way it was, the way it will be. But there's also stinking thinking that you can shift if you are lucky, or you have the bottle. That will come later.

There is definitely something about Easter in Ireland. Resurrection. Gorse blossom, spring lambs, chocolate eggs for rolling, and revolution, all stirred together. The result is enigmatic, like iffy gelignite. And people do odd things. Or they seem odd from the outside, until you get the story. Because nothing is as it seems. Add in moonshine and you'll see old codgers creeping from the shelter of rocks, casting yesterday's shadows in their carpet slippers, but gravitating, like land-crabs, toward the din of battle. Even if it's just a memory.

And so it was on that snowy Saturday that the great Jinxie McDevitt, and the rest of the patriots were set to take the Post Office, for the year that was in it, on account of being pros. Old pros. God, most of us were grandparents. But we would ignore arthritic limbs, would truss up and keep pace with The Jinx's navy blue, sliding doors Berlingo, to the nods of his threadbare tiger in the back window. It would be momentous, with Jinxie himself at the helm again, in this crazy solo run.

We would go 'straight in, but stay cool,' as Jinxie put it at the planning session. 'No messing and nobody does a runner, do you hear me, Danny Boy Fox?' Danny Boy worked shifts in 'The Crib', an old men's bar. He used to be quick with his mitts, but his blood pressure, and lack of practice, was an issue. Everybody had been hand-picked by The Jinx, but it was a no-brainer. The whole gang was going to be back. It would be a poetic heist, he said. A renewal of vows. Like Theo had held for his marriage to Isobel after forty years. A new evocation, Jinxie said. Each of us would look out for the other, as comrades. We were all equal. Aye, right.

'No bother,' said Danny Boy, before he knew the score. He was to be responsible for Big Eugene, who had pretended, let's face it,' The Jinx said, 'for a full generation, to be… simple.' The onset of simplicity having set in directly after our last big job. That was a lifetime ago. We thought we had retired. Naturally, Danny was sweating, having harmlessly served Mackesons for eighteen years. But now The Jinx had put the bite on him and he was feeling it. We all were. Especially Eugene.

'Eugene's your baby,' said The Jinx to Danny. He was beaming like Satan. Some bleeding baby. Eugene was six-foot-two, sixty-five years old, and apt to cry. Because of trauma – and Danny knew it, but he couldn't, wouldn't take on The Jinx. At that point, we were all the same.

Eugene was to carry the actual bomb. Everything would be symbolic. Phoenixes rising. The year? 2016. The day? Spot on. Well damned near it. The target? Okay, it wasn't the GPO but it would be open for business. Fair enough, it wasn't Dublin, but the cause was the same. Éire Nua. And why? Because the wee black North was still detached. Two-thirds of the fourth field. Or was there something else? There's always a subplot, right?

Early on I knew it was payback time for Eugene.

Danny would have a tricky job with him, given Eugene's dependence on diazepam, but his role would be crucial for certain, historical reasons, which were not in the history books but were familiar to Jinxie who, like an elephant, always remembered stuff, VERY WELL indeed.

Let's say that Eugene was not exactly The Jinx's favourite ex-quartermaster. True, he'd somehow left us all bare-arsed. We'd never got to the bottom of it but we thought The Jinx had let it slide. Not so. 'Frig's sake,' was all Danny said when he was recommissioned. You didn't muck about with The Jinx. That was a well-known secret. For myself, I said, just kept an eye on Danny.

That was us then: Jinxie, Danny, Eugene and me. There was also Paddy No Thumbs – don't ask – Bosco Quigley Senior, who had been our sniper, and bomber Theo (real name Shugh). He was living in a Fold, where he got no grief. But he told Jinxie that he couldn't wait to get stuck in. He lied. We were all ex-killers and a great bunch of fellas, according to The Jinx.

That was, except for Eugene. Well, what could Jinxie say about a 'volunteer who had handed us weapons that jammed? All of them, and not just the handguns.' At the very least it was carelessness. No wonder Eugene sought refuge in madness.

Jinxie had done the longest stretch, being the leader. He had gone in, and come out bitter. The rest of us got lighter sentences, because nobody was shot. And then, after Good Friday, we all got out. It was happy days, relatively speaking.

For years, Jinxie had been keeping an allotment, growing spears of asparagus, like Percy Thrower, but he'd sworn that he'd trap Eugene in the long grass, like a big floppy rabbit. When he wouldn't be thinking. It would all be in the timing. And impact.

Eugene had fell to bits. When people started a collection for him outside the chapel, he brought in more in than the Knights of Malta, and that got right up The Jinx's nose.

So anyway, 2016 was the big memorial year, when Jinxie got it all together.

There was a night in 'The Crib', when it all kicked off. I was there myself. So far, it had been a right good wee evening, with Jimmy O'D vamping on the organ. Not too loud.

At least you could talk. Danny looked the part with the oul linen apron on him. There was only two women in the bar.

You weren't allowed to smoke, but hey. It was blue fug and peanuts. If you haven't been to The Crib, it's an honest-to-God bar full of dropped bellies and sweaty oxters. You'll see a lot of red faces, and numbed men stumbling over stools. But there's never any hassle.

Or there wasn't then. Old comrades.

'Sorry, mate,' they say, when they spill your drink, 'just need to go out behind.'

'Out behind' is a concrete bunker with no electric, a single urinal, sog and butts. But it's yellow and familiar. And full bladders can't be choosy. You can take it easy there. No call to slash and dash. The rusty cisterns sit high and haughty. To be fair, they've seen it all. There's a comforting stench.

Eugene, God help him, was avoiding the drinkers, debating two sides of an argument with… himself. It seemed to be about Ruairí somebody, a helicopter and a Morris Avenger. He was mumbling, as usual, into his Pepsi, doing no harm to nobody. Too scared to talk out loud, and too terrified to be on his own, but we knew the drill. The boys had got over his mistake and The Crib seemed like a safe space.

Danny's measures were dodgy. You didn't complain but it made you think. There was no ice but he kept a fire burning. Cheap Polish coal. Above the grate was a wrinkled picture of Pearse and a copy of the Proclamation, both hanging crooked.

The two females were on the game. They were just a couple of girls, getting ready to go out. 'What are youse doing in here for the Rising?' asked Evelyn, checking her mascara.

'We'll toast your man up there,' said Danny, pointing at Pearse. It wasn't the most respectful.

'That's a sin,' said Evelyn, applying her lip gloss, 'themuns were real men and martyrs.'

'We did our bit,' said Danny, 'what have you ever done for Ireland?' There was no call for that.

'Plenty,' said Evelyn, buttoning her coat. 'Give us another Bacardi, for the central heating. Would you look at that poor fella there,' she said, looking at Eugene.

Eugene groaned.

'Is that what freedom fighting did for him?' she said. 'No offence.'

I was just going to play the fruit machine, when Knees McNabb came in with Toby, his terrier, on a length of string. Knees was very great with The Jinx. His eyes and ears.

'What about you, Knees,' we said, making room for him, 'and you too, Toby?'

'Toby needs a high stool,' said Knees. 'He's bate out. Him and me's been up the thingamy.'

'Good memories, eh?' said Danny, setting him up one. Knees fluttered the same blue fiver with the tear in it that he always flashed. The one he kept for bars.

'Away to hell,' said Danny, 'are you codding?'

'Fair play,' said Knees, stashing it back in his pocket for the next time. 'Give us a saucer.' He split the Mackeson between himself and the dog. Toby was lapping it up.

'How many was it?' some fool whispered. What sort of question was that?

Knees looked at Eugene.

'He's only out of the big house again,' Danny said, letting on to be concerned. 'He's lost in space.'

'Well, he'd better come back to earth quick,' said Knees, smacking his lips, 'because youse are about to get a wee visit.'

This was bad news. Eugene was eating his fingers.

'You're all right, pet,' said Assumpta, Evelyn's mate. 'Nobody's holding nothing against you.'

'I wouldn't be too sure about that,' said Knees, looking up at Pearse, 'I'm sure youse are doing something for the centenary?'

'Yeah, yeah,' said Danny.

'Proper order,' said Knees. 'Well, have a good one. Toby needs a pee.'

'Take him out the back,' said the D man.

'I've more respect for a dumb animal,' said Knees. 'Good luck.'

Knees was the angel of death. That was the night we knew we were put on standby. It would be only a matter of time.

After he left, nobody was talking, except Eugene. I could still smell the trail of the girls. Danny stood behind the bar, faraway, back in time, rewashing glasses. The big fella was all over the place, with his voices all yammering at once. People have their own torture to bear, but his was worse than most. It was wait and see.

We didn't have to long to wait. It was Jinxie himself that brought us together, upstairs in 'The Sicily', like old times, but most of us used the lift.

'So, here we are again, Danny,' he said in his steely voice. 'And what about the boul Eugene, still gibbering?' There had never been a bead of compassion with The Jinx.

Eugene had stopped his fussing.

'See, there you are,' said The Jinx, 'he can damned well stop it when he likes.' It was spooky listening to him. Like some old teacher's nails scraping a blackboard.

'It's going to be classical,' he said.

Things would definitely be different this time. It was to be low-tech. The foot soldiers would dander up X Avenue (Jinxie was speaking in code). 'Youse will look like you're going to buy Chum,' he said.

I was to give out the shooters and masks the night before. Eugene wouldn't carry a weapon.

'You will have tested them all,' The Jinx told me. 'Discretely.' Not as easy as it sounded. He was watching Eugene. I would be watching Danny. Bosco and Paddy were all right. We would supply the cover. We had 250 years among us. It was *Dad's Army*, but it wasn't British, and nobody was laughing.

'Theo and me will arrive last in the Berlingo, and park in the wee lay-by,' Jinxie said. 'The rest of youse will have taken up positions. Danny you'll be ready with your man. Have youse all got that? You will walk Eugene, nice and slow to the car, Danny, to get "Maria"' – that's what we used to call the bombs – 'which I have made myself.'

'Is it a big one?' asked Bosco.

'It's not some poxy wee fruit cake' said The Jinx. 'It will be in a Spar bag. And you'll carry it the right way up,' he said to Eugene. 'I've went to a lot of bother over it, for our country. There'll be no cock ups this time.'

'Got you,' said Paddy.

Eugene whimpered. The old fear was in Danny's eyes, and I wondered – he'd always been jittery on active service. There was a lot you didn't know.

The Jinx's eyes were shining with his plan. They were lit up with hate. But there's hate and hate. He loved reprisals. I looked round the room. A bunch of oldies you'd have seen at a tea dance. Nobody including me, was taking him on. Not in The Sicily. And not then.

Eugene's eyes twitched. His slobber was back at the thought of carrying Maria with Danny's pistol in his back. It was pure sadism. It was also right out of *Blue Peter*. But we didn't say.

'What about the staff and customers?' I asked.

'I'll see,' said The Jinx. 'Remember, post offices are the state. Even on days when they're not selling stamps.'

'That's it,' said Theo.

Bosco and Paddy were doing rightly. It was killing Danny. I wasn't sure why, but I was pleased. Eugene sobbed in big, marshmallow gasps.

'Shut him the hell up,' said The Jinx, 'he should have thought about all this when he was working for the Brits.'

'What?' we said. It was balls. There was no way. Eugene wailed. Danny spread out his hands.

'Well,' said The Jinx, 'what else?' There can be a terrible cruelty in the smile of an old man. He had loved killing people. And he wasn't done. Knowledge was power, and Jinx knew a lot. 'Who ever heard of all the guns going on the blink on the same night?' he said. 'We'll be giving a reminder to touts and toadies.'

The bloody war was supposed to be over.

'Me and Theo will wait in the car,' said Jinxie. 'Danny goes in with Eugene and shouts, "Bomb," like we used to. Then comrade Eugene here will calmly place it on the counter, do youse hear me, beside the driving licence application forms. There's plenty of room. Because I've checked. Now, here's the good bit. Eugene will stay behind in the wee post office, in the cause of Irish freedom, for the count of ten. Can you count that far, Eugene? You'll do it slowly. If he comes out too quick, you will shoot him, Danny, between the eyes. Are you with me? I'm using a new timer, and it will be bang on, if you get me. Bob will be your uncle, as they say, and Fanny, Eugene, will be your aunt.'

'Frig's sake, Jinxie,' said Danny.

'Have youse fuckin' got it?' said The Jinx.

Bosco was trembling. He was waiting for a hip replacement.

The Jinx and Theo would be away in the Berlingo, while the rest of us would pocket our masks and 'melt away' like they do in the movies. Eugene could go to hell. If he wasn't blew up. This was one man's dirty war. There was method in it. But it wasn't right.

On Good Friday evening, I did the Stations, wore the lily, and said a prayer. After a fish from Bridie's, I went round the lads with the guns. I'd discharged them in a cushion up the back lane. God knows where The Jinx had dug them up, but they were perfect. It was freezing cold, because Easter was early and there were a few flurries of snow.

I went round the boys on foot. The moon was just off circle.

The boys looked pale. They said they wouldn't sleep. Danny had nothing to say. By the time I reached home, big proper flakes were falling.

I didn't sleep either, I kept thinking back. Searching my mind but I couldn't pin it. I had called at Eugene's as well. I'd wanted to talk to him. To some way mark his card. But his blinds were down.

I battered his door. He was in there on his own, all right, because he had nobody. But he was sitting tight. He'd be up for Danny in the morning. I tried to imagine what it was like to be him. To be a living reminder to yourself of failure, and I couldn't. I wasn't making a fortune on the taxis, but I was doing okay. And I didn't beat myself up about the past. Why should I? War was war.

But, hey, this was different. The children had made a snowman at his front. They'd written in the snow, in great big letters – oh my God. 'Spastic Santa'. And it was Good Friday. All through the night it had snowed. I knew, because I was in and out of sleep, dreaming of Jinxie on the steps of the Post Office reading the Proclamation. His words came out in a jumble. In the dreams, I could see Eugene's head detached from his neck, going out of focus, like the Cheshire Cat, but there was no smile. Only blood dripping through his thin hair, and collecting in the dark crevasses of his skin. And I could see Danny's gun. At times it was loaded and then it was empty. Sometimes it was going off and sometimes when he pulled the trigger, there was nothing in the chamber. I woke at six, wondering, and asking how in the name of God a pensioner of seventy-two could still have us all by the short hairs?

A text, from The Jinx.

'Daffodils.'

More of his codes. It was on. I don't know how many inches of snow there was, that morning, in fairyland.

I made a strong coffee and sat in my nags, smoking, and figuring what to do. There weren't many options. We were now a geriatric execution gang. My fingers played with the new Nokia I'd got. I looked at the spring photos they send you. Real daffodils. A wee lad in round glasses, holding a black lamb on a lead at the front of the city hall. It was a great snap.

Eugene could probably have broken Danny's neck. But he hadn't. His head was down. They were standing in the lay-by, waiting for the Berlingo. Danny was circling him like a hyena. Bosco and No Thumbs were in position. I could see their tracks in the snow, where they'd dragged their feet. It was one of those mornings when all the sound is sucked from the world, and you're in a vacuum.

In the end, though it was late, I'd made the call. And it hurt like hell. Blowing the whistle on your old mates is pure shite. But The Jinx was bigger shite.

They would catch the Berlingo before the shops. I should have done it earlier. I'd told them about the timer.

A brick lorry wheezed up the hill, its back wheels spinning. People weren't used to snow.

We looked at our watches. Paddy No Thumbs, Bosco Quigley Senior and me.

In the lay-by, Danny the warder stamped his feet, like a guard keeping warm.

Eugene just waited; a big tame wolf, panting out air from his lungs. He was silent now, knowing it would soon be over. The Jinx had lived up to his name.

And then the bang. That went on and on...

The snow must have beaten Jinxie. He should have called it off. The Berlingo had let him down? No good on ice? He'd run out of rope before they even got to him. He was sliding all over the road. Had to be. The timer had been too sharp. He'd been past his best.

I collected the guns from the boys. 'Now split,' I said.

'Gimmie yours, you bastard,' I said to Danny. The more I thought about him, the more I wasn't sure. But it didn't matter now. Like I say, Easter had always been more than chicks and bunnies. It brought death and miracles. Pearse knew that. We got our own miracle a hundred years later. The Berlingo was passing the park when it went up, and there was nobody about. Thanks be to Almighty God. But there's always collateral.

'Come on, Eugene,' I said.

Poor oul Theo was the sacrifice this time. We went to the wake. His wee cramped Fold was stuffed, what with Isobel and their five grand-weans. They were all torn to fragments. It was heartbreaking. Danny was just leaving, but I let him go. I could have been wrong.

Maybe it really was all over now. I was glad to see Evelyn and Assumpta. Eugene was back on the wards. Some funerals you don't attend. I didn't go to Jinxie's.

Moon Strikers

I'm only off the plane from the mess that is Aleppo. I haven't shaved. First stop, Aunt Marsha.

'If I could bottle you up, I'd sell you and make a fortune,' I used to tell her.

'Like jolly pots of jam,' she'd said one time. 'Then people could spread me on their bread and eat me up.'

There was the Colonel, walking to the reinforced glass door of Ardshee Quality Nursing Home. I pressed the bell where it said 'Ring'. The Colonel was in his usual green blazer and regimental tie – I thought he looked thinner – directing his regiment of stooped females, marshalling them like ducks, in the foyer. The women fussed round him, waving wasted old limbs like sticks. Aunt Marsha, God save us, was not like them.

A nurse scythed through the swarm, holding a swipe card. I waited for the buzzer. The Colonel frowned when he saw me. 'Absent without leave again, Sergeant,' he said, 'prepare to face a charge.'

'Special assignment,' I said, 'four months in the Middle East.'

'Bloody powder keg,' he said. 'I blame the brass.' He raised one arm to shake my hand. 'Lost the other somewhere. Probably in the Congo.'

I waited for the next bit.

'Damned awkward in the jacks, I'll tell you that.'

172

His routine meant something to him.

'Let this man through,' he barked. The women scattered like sparrows.

'All clear,' he said, 'pass on.' The strength of his voice had always surprised me.

'How's tricks?' I said to the nurse. 'How is my favourite aunt?' The nurse looked down. 'Mrs B would like a word before you go up.'

Mrs Bratton was the newish matron. In charge a month when I'd flown out. Marsha had loved the last woman.

'What's eating her?' I said.

'Ah now,' said the nurse.

The matron's office was a square, glass tank. Mrs B stared through its transparent walls like a fish in an aquarium. Marsha called her 'the Shark'.

'Maybe you're being too quick,' I said.

'I'll give her a month,' she'd told me, 'no need for a judge and jury.'

'She's not herself, Mr… eh?' The Shark didn't bother with the names of relatives. 'Aren't you the only kin? You haven't been around much.'

'Didn't I tell you I'd be away?' I said. It wasn't a great start.

She didn't reply.

'I was in touch every week,' I told her. 'Marsha hates the phone. The girls on duty said she was grand.'

'*Grand* can cover a multitude of sins,' said the Shark.

'If there was some hassle, you should have let me know,' I said. 'I left you my mobile number. What's the story anyway? She was in good heart when I left.'

'She's not eating,' she said. 'You'll see a change in her. She has become paranoid and irrational.'

'It could be the urinary tract again,' I said. 'Does she have a temperature? She was like that in her own house. Drinking out of coasters. Is she on an antibiotic? Did you get the doctor for her?'

'It's the dementia,' she said, 'and naughtiness.'

To hell with naughtiness.

'She makes up stories,' said the Shark, 'which are nasty and vicious.'

'That's not like Marsha at all,' I said, taking a good look at the Shark.

'She'll destroy the reputation of this home,' she said. 'The inspection people believe every fairy tale they're told. You'll need to speak to her and get her to stop talking nonsense or she'll have to be moved.'

'Tell her to wise up, is it?' I said.

The corridor to Marsha's room smelled like a pine forest. With an underlying hint of something unpleasant. They must have been fairly splashing out on the air freshener anyway. Ardshee's mission statement was plastered everywhere. 'Ageing with Dignity.' Just the job.

My aunt was snoring in the chair beside her bed. The crocheted blanket I had picked up for her at a craft fair was lying at her feet. Not the cleanest. Neither was the carpet. I tucked the blanket around her knees. Grubby and all as it was. Her mouth was wide open. The dentures hung loose. I felt the radiator. Tepid. She jumped when I touched her wrist. Her skin was cool. 'Can I turn down the tele?' I said, reaching for the remote. 'It's making an awful racket.'

'Oh, it's you,' she said, 'Television is drivel. Sit down where I can see you.' She pointed to the other seat. There were stains on her face and her floral dress. Maybe it was brown sauce.

'I thought you were dead,' she said. 'You look a bit puffy. I hope you're not overdoing the whiskey. Where have you been gallivanting?'

'Out foreign for *The Times*,' I told her. 'I was on the blower a lot of times to see how you were doing.'

'Is that a joke?' she said. 'They tell me nothing. The Great White has the rest of them as bad as herself. The whole place will soon be in the Marianas Trench. You recall Mr O'Riordan? Well, he disappeared. Spirited away. Where is he now? No one knows. He might be shot or dumped for speaking out.'

'About what?' I asked.

'The bruise on his head.'

'What happened to him?'

'I'm saying nothing.'

'How have you been?' I said, keeping the coat on. 'Are you warm enough in here?'

'Well, since you ask,' she said, 'I have gone right off this hotel, since *she* came. She won't burn the oil but I was never used to heat, so that's all right.'

I took her hands. They were cold.

'Do you still believe in morality?' she asked. 'I was telling the Colonel, it's like a farmyard in this place. A woman climbs into my bed, when I am in it, with the light out and my prayers said. It's as well I wear pyjamas. She's looking for her Persian tom. It's called Ahmad. Well, it won't be sleeping with me and neither will she.'

'Is there no one with any sense?' I asked. 'Does the priest come at all?'

'Are you mad?' she said, 'They are in on the whole thing. I've tried to talk about it to the man next door. He's all right, but he's a Protestant. It's a waste of time. He stands all day at the lift in his gabardine, waiting for the Dublin bus. It never comes. Put your head around the corner now and take a look. Go on. He looks normal, but he's well below par up there, if you ask me.'

'So, there's no banter at all now?' I said. 'Just crazy people doing daft things. God, and you were always a great one for the craic.'

'It's become too dismal,' she said. 'Would you pour me a drink? The dining room is the worst. If you don't eat your lunch you get no dinner. That can't be right when you're paying for it. You should see how emaciated some of the women are. Give me an educated man every time,' she said. 'Dr Osgood sits at my table. He has a beautiful accent but a terrible shake. He still performs a few little operations, to stop him from getting rusty. Did you know he once gave that Presley fellow a ball and socket?'

'He'd be worth a few bob,' I said.

'Are you keen on money?' she asked. 'It's no use to me at my age. Anyway, they take it out of your purse.'

'Who's doing that?'

'Oh everyone,' she said. 'It's for the Shark slush fund. Shush, not a word.'

'Where is your purse?' I asked her.

'I'm not telling you,' she said. 'I have it hidden. I wouldn't please them. Elvis had plenty of lolly, you know, and a fat lot of good it did him. The doctor says he was addicted to cookies – that's how Americans refer to biscuits.'

'You get all sorts in here all right,' I said. 'What about the physiotherapy lad that took a shine to you?'

'He's a pervert,' she said. 'I told them all about him but they laughed.'

'I brought you a few grapes,' I told her. 'Is green all right? Do you want me to wash them? Is that a tap running somewhere? There's a fierce noise of water.'

'It's the new woman, next door,' she said. 'Flushing Florrie. *She* shouts at her. But it makes no difference. Florrie believes that snakes wiggle out of the sewer pipes, into her bum.'

'You wouldn't want that,' I said. 'Sure didn't St Patrick get rid of those divils, years ago. And you tell me they shout at her for that?'

'It's only a fixation,' she said. 'That's what they call any stupid notion nowadays. She can't help it.'

'No ordinary five-eights at all,' I said.

'We have a farmer,' she said. 'His moustache is like a dead gerbil. It filters debris. The waitresses used to pick bits of vegetable out of it after the soup, but they have no time now. He shares his Liquorice Allsorts, but he's gaga. Everyone is. I suppose he used to be a decent spud.'

'How are you doing with the food?' I asked.

'I can feed myself, so I don't starve,' she said. 'Do you still have your own teeth? You would need tusks like a walrus to munch through the stuff they give you these days. Last week a child from the technical college made breakfast. He said he hadn't "did eggs yet". Imagine. We had rubber toast without them.'

'And the women are loopy too?'

'We have some freaks,' she said. 'The tallest woman in the world lives here. They call her "wee pet". Have you lost your wee fork? Wee was not a dictionary word when I was at school, and it is not used in a kind way.'

'How do you mean?' I said.

'I'm not saying,' she said.

'Well, I see they got you a Honda Fifty anyway,' I said, trying the brakes of the maroon rollator parked in the corner.

'I'm not allowed to use it,' she said, 'because I won't do aerobics. But I won't give in. "We'll have you ready for the Olympic Games," they tell you. What rot.'

Then Marsha lowered her voice. 'I'm going to share something top secret,' she said. 'Bar that door. It's classified information.'

'It won't lock,' I said, 'but I'll shut it tight.'

'Right,' she said. 'Cross your heart and hope to die?'

'Go for it,' I said.

'I'm leaving,' she said. 'I bet you didn't know that. I've had enough.'

'Is the Colonel in on it?' I asked.

'I think so,' she said. 'I saw a woman being dragged across the floor.'

'Did you now?' my eyes were on her wispy hair. 'Has that ever happened to you?'

'No fear,' she said. 'The woman was squealing. I'm damned well going. Most of us are. "Inhuman treatment", that's what it's called.'

'Tell me more,' I say. She shrank at the sound of approaching footsteps. Whoever it was, walked past.

'You are only supposed to move your bowels once a day,' she said. 'Hard luck on you if you ask twice. In my experience bowels have a mind of their own, so there will be accidents. How would you like that?'

I felt myself shudder. 'Can I get you something warmer to put around you?' I said, riffling through her wardrobe. Old heavy skirts and tweed.

'It's worse than a concentration camp,' she said.

'This isn't sounding good at all, Marsha,' I told her.

'We'll attract world headlines,' she said, 'but there's a news embargo at present. After we cut loose and blow town, then you may go to print. When the horse has bolted.'

'When's all this happening?'

'Next full moon,' she said. 'I've formed an escape committee. We're standing by. Torches, maps, iron rations in lockers.'

'You've thought of everything.'

'And we got rid of the ditherers,' she beamed. 'We're down to hardcore, backbone and breeding. No hangers on. I knew a college boy once. We had lovely picnics with hampers and cold meats. Then he went off to Trinity and that was that. Nothing ever stays the same.'

'Are you planning reprisals?' I said.

'No decision yet,' she said. 'We are not the Nazi party or Stalin's crowd. But you-know-who and her gang will get the chop. Did you know that the noisy people are given pills to shut them up? She made Mr Dempsey take a bath in cold water because he was looking at rude pictures. Men are all like that, they can't help it. Your father was the same. She deserves the death penalty. We will run her over with zimmers. "Good riddance," I say.'

'No messing.'

'You'll have your scoop, don't worry,' she said. 'I hope you work for a proper paper. Precision is the watchword. No sloppy adverbs. Readers require the truth. There now.' She sat back in the Parker Knoll, drained. 'I need a cup of tea,' she said.

'Let me find a spare waitress,' I said. 'I'll take a bit of a walk.'

'Well, tell them I want to spend a penny.'

'Have you any digestives for an oul dunk?' I asked the care woman when she brought in the tray.

'I haven't,' she said. 'We've scrapped them. They're not good for the old ones. Mrs Bratten says we're cutting back.'

'I don't like the name we have chosen,' Marsha said, when your woman left. 'You'll laugh. It's the Baked Beans.'

'Baked Beans Break Out,' I said. 'Well, it has the alliteration, anyway.'

'Rubbish,' she said, 'Moon Strikers would have been much better. It was a group decision. I'll expect you to give us a proper headline.'

'You're safe enough with me,' I said. 'I'll do a thorough job on the whole thing.'

'Just be careful,' she said, 'and watch your back.'

'Don't worry,' I said.

'Reach me a Kleenex,' she said. 'My eyes have started this watering business. I hope it won't be a problem when we are on the run.' The room hadn't warmed. Marsha was drooping.

'I must say you have behaved all right, for a press man,' she told me, fiddling with her glasses. 'It will be your upbringing. You do resemble your father, but he was better looking. I hope I can trust you with all of this.'

'A hundred per cent,' I said.

'Then let yourself out,' she said. 'I need a doze.'

The Shark's sonar was finely tuned. She spotted me approaching the closed door of her tank, her chin receding to infinity. She emerged, blinking.

'Did you talk to her then?' she asked.

'Oh yes,' I said.

'And you agree it's a worry?'

'I certainly do,' I said. 'There's no doubt about it.'

'Well, that's something,' she said, 'some relatives refuse to take things seriously.'

'You'll not find that with me,' I told her.

'You get families that never see a problem,' she said.

'I'm sure you do. Not guilty, Mrs Bratten,' I said. 'I'll not be sitting on my hands but I'll need to take advice on the best way to skin the cat, so to speak, before I can take action. If you know what I mean. Taking everything into consideration, and that.'

The Shark had begun to nod, but she'd picked up a tremor in the water. The two tiny glass eyes glinted deep in her face.

'I've recorded what she told me,' I said.

'You are supposed to ask first,' she said.

'In here,' I said, pointing to my brain. 'It's called recall. A gift I got from her side of the tribe. She could buy and sell us all.'

'We have to be careful,' she said. 'They all tell stories.'

'I do the same myself,' I said. 'And I'm always careful. It's my training.'

'What do you do?' asked the Shark in her deep-water voice.

'I'm with a paper,' I said. 'I cover Syria.'

'Syria,' she said, looking blank.

'Yeah, it's a war zone.'

'Very good,' she said, slowly, her lips rolling back to expose two rows of teeth. Fins trembling, she wafted me to the door. 'I'm sure we can sort it out,' she said.

'Are you, Mrs Bratten?' I said. 'I hope are you are right, and I hope you have been listening. Her room is freezing, you'll have to turn up the heat.'

'There'll be an air lock in the system,' she said.

'I don't care what's in the system,' I said. 'She needs more therms. You know, like energy. And more blankets on her bed. Clean ones. I want you to wash her dress at sixty degrees, and bin that dog blanket.

That's for openers. Are you getting me?'

She squinted at me from behind her spectacles. Like she had just spotted a bigger fish. 'Staff,' she oozed, 'I need to be on their backs all the time. Seniors can't tell what's fact or fiction.'

'You tell me that,' I said, 'but I can, and so can my paper. Don't think for a second that an old one doesn't know the difference between care and neglect because she's doting.'

'We don't say that in here,' she said.

'Do we not?' I said.

'It's the wrong language,' she said.

'It will go in *The Times*,' I said, 'for the readers, along with a nice likeness of yourself.'

'Oh God,' she said.

'That's right,' I said. 'Oh God. Do you ever say your prayers at all? I'll be back to do the job right.'

'I see,' she said. 'So that's the way of it? You won't find anything…'

'That's great,' I said, heading for the door.

'Mission accomplished, Sergeant?' asked the Colonel, still at his post. There wasn't a pick on him.

'Staking out today,' I told him. 'Reconnaissance before attack. You know yourself. Battle stations tomorrow.'

'Proper order,' he said, 'and you're well on track?'

'Affirmative,' I said. 'We have the enemy in our sights. Just going to assemble the men.'

'Good man,' he said, straightening the tie. 'Stay sharp. A bayonet in the arse is what they want, the lazy buggers. Then tails up, what?'

'You're with us then?' I asked.

'Too ripe for action now,' he said, 'otherwise I'd be your man. I'd be in there with you, like a shot. I served in Cyprus. I know what's going on. I miss nothing, you know. A sentry's job. Poor show. Bad standards.'

'Can you give supporting fire?' I said.

'Bloody sure,' he said, sneaking a look at the Shark's window. 'Launch the landing craft, and good fishing.'

'Good on you,' I said.

The Shark treaded water. 'I'll be back,' I say. 'Soon.' Her gills pulsed in and out. I stepped outside and looked back at Ardshee: at the high brick walls, the narrow windows and the slack faces almost visible behind the glass. I could see Marsha's room at the western end. She was one of sixty. The Colonel was waving now, calling me back, and sounding urgent.

'No monkey business,' he whispered, clearing his old clogged throat, 'and get that hair cut, sonny. It's a bad example to the chaps.'

Drumming

My name is Hooch Gillespie. Okay, I've had my issues. This here happened during the first Covid summer, right? You were allowed to be inside with people but you were supposed to be careful. Masks were optional. Me and Packie, that's my best and only mate, are at the wee writing class in the Catwater Library. It's mixed. Religion's still important in the city. You always need to know who you're with, but everybody's on the level. As far as we know anyway. Isolation's a real bummer. So, thank God for something that gets you out.

I'm a Prod. Packie's a Catholic. No worries. Him and me's the same age. Fifty. We met at the Technical School. Not yesterday. Fifty. Imagine. The Techs stayed mixed. It's a long story, but we found out that our two mothers were killed by the same bomb, the one that blew up Cowdry's clothes shop, when we were youngsters. They didn't know each other. It was pure coincidence.

Neither of us is going with anybody. Pat's our group leader and she's great. We don't know what she is. But that's okay, because she has to be neutral. Anyhow, it doesn't matter because she's from outside our divided 'enclave'. That's what they call it on the news. We all know each other's names by now. Names are the sure giveaway. Friendship before tribe is a good motto, but all the same.

'Everybody's back again,' Pat says, giving us her welcome smile. 'This is marvellous, have you all been busy writing?' Maybe she sounds a bit over the top, but actually, she means it. Pat's dead on.

We're separated out round the big oval table upstairs, in the open space with the windows wedged wide, for ventilation. It's first week in July, and it's been a great spell of weather.

'So, who's going to lead off this week?' Pat says, very gentle. I never wrote before this club. Only shopping lists.

It's your Spanish girl with the freckles, that always sits on Packie's right, that wants to go first, and Michael the old English guy, says 'A volunteer's worth half a dozen conscripts,' which means he could have been in the army, and maybe married a woman here.

The Spanish doll's called Therese. The Spanish are all Catholics. She's wearing a red mask with wee stars on it, like the ones I never got at school. She's sitting closer than she should to Packie, but he's not complaining. He's loving it. I'm not bloody blind.

It's a small group, but that's okay. There's a hairdresser called Delores, say no more, Beth, a wee religious dental nurse from McLister Street, and big pale Cyril, with the diabetes – both Prods. He writes about space travel. There's Ruthie who works in 'The Last Man Standing', which is not a bad bar – also a Prod – as well as Packie and me. So, that's a decent spread. At least you know where you are. Except for the Englishman, who could be anything.

'It's crime isn't it,' Pat says to Therese.

You don't have to read your stuff out if you can't face it, because it can spook you. But if you chicken out it makes you feel like shit. That there's what it does to me, anyway.

Delores writes frilly romance. That's what she says. The Englishman worked in the shipyard, so he's into cranes and welding. Wee Beth's depressed. Doesn't like being off work and she's worried about her son, who's always getting beat up. She talked to me about him at the bus stop. It's because he's odd. She hasn't read out anything yet. Ruthie says she's a nature writer. Fair enough. I'm working on a story about Skinner Street, where I live, if you could call it living, in the smallest flat in Ulster.

I keep telling Packie that him and me don't need women. We have each other. We're not gay, but we have a deep thing going on.

The windows are open. There's not supposed to be a Twelfth this year, but you can hear the Lambegs warming up. People beating the hell out of them in their backyards. Nobody says nothing about the drums at the group, because you don't. Not when you're with Catholics. You hear them with a different part of your brain. You don't know what they're hearing – how could you – and you don't ask. That's how it works for everyone. Except me and Packie.

I don't know if I like whodunnits. Maybe you read a lot. I'm only getting into it. At my school nobody read anything. I'm really slow, five pages an hour, but I don't say that out loud. Packie says I'll pick up speed, but I don't know. I like stories about lions. There was a fella down our way that used to keep one in a hut, but a guy shot it. He said it was a man-eater.

I always think I can smell my own sweat at the class, but there's a handy breeze blowing through, so that's cool.

Therese is shaking a bit, which surprises me, her being a teacher and all. Just shows you. Packie says it doesn't matter what you work at, you tremble when you read your own stuff. That's because you're putting yourself on the line. And if you don't, you're not getting it, because you write out of your soul. He doesn't need to shake. He's always composing these brilliant poems about birds. He has a thing about swans. Me and him dander down by the ponds, which are halfway between Skinner Street and St Brigid's Drive, where he hangs out. I can't go to his house and he can't come to mine, for obvious reasons. Look at the colour of the kerbstones and you'll see why. That's the way it is. Everything's divided.

'What's the name of your main character, Therese?' Pat says.

'It starts with Miguel,' she says. You'd know she was a foreigner, but you can make her out. 'There are many protagonists...'

A protagonist's a character. Right? What the hell?

'I would like to have written it in Spanish but...'

Thank God she didn't.

'Maybe someday, Therese,' Pat says, 'when we've all had lessons. I'm afraid most of us in this place are not the greatest linguists.'

Too right.

'And now that we're leaving Europe... But we'll not go there. Let's settle down, and hear a good murder story.'

Therese's eyelids flicker. Her story's typed and all. I'm no good with bloody plots. I never know what's going to happen. I was the only one who hadn't heard of *The Mousetrap*. I'm going to be lost in no time. She's getting ready. There's a bit of shouting outside. There's supposed to be no gatherings. Somebody's playing a flute.

She clears her throat. 'Here we go. It is market day in the northern town', she says. 'The grey-haired Miguel has a good fruit stall. There are many stalls. He sells red apples and Sevilles – wee sour oranges – and there are melons, also. The town women stroll, meander, filling baskets with fresh breads, buying olives, thinking of their sons and husbands, if they would like this or that, smiling at the faces of the other *señoras*, glad maybe, they are not so fat as they. Such thoughts go through their minds.

'In the middle of the stalls, Miguel, who looks too old to have a child, is busy with his young daughter Laura. Perhaps she is ten. They make churros, a kind of pastry, melting chocolate on a tiny spirit stove, laughing about something private. They are close. A floppy dog named Roberto keeps his head down. He has fleas and sniffs for scraps, the way dogs do. Lifting his leg because he is a boy – she gets a laugh. 'A butcher throws him trimmings, is that the word? Midday. The sun is the devil in a cobalt sky. Just another Monday in the Basque Country.'

So, where is this Basque Country? I thought we were in Spain. And who's gonna be the criminal? Maybe I'm missing something. Packie's eyes are on Therese's smooth arms. I can see him. He definitely fancies her. The story's all right so far. Not too complicated. Maybe nothing has actually happened yet. It could be interesting. I wouldn't mind a churro.

'A pair of storks nest in the spire of the church of Santa Maria de la Antigua. They have new chicks. Scraps of fluff on long thin legs. The church bell tolls. The traders drink *café con leche* and smoke. Men spit flakes of Moroccan tobacco, rearrange *un poco* their pots and pans. The devil glints on their kettles. Old women buy lace mantillas and crucifixes, children spin circles in the street, dancing around and around until they're dizzy. Sitting cross-legged, a love-struck gypsy boy strums guitar. Two priests are about to hear confessions... Bless me, Padre.'

There's a lot of priests in Spain.

Therese looks at Pat. 'You want me to read more?'

'Oh, there's no perhaps about it, Therese,' Pat says, 'we have to hear it all.'

There has to be a murder weapon. Who's going to get killed and what's the motive? Maybe I'm even thicker than I thought. Keep calm, I tell myself. There's a lot of traffic out there Covid or no Covid.

'Is it too noisy?' Pat asks, 'we can close the windows a little.'

Therese is on the edge of her green plastic chair. She wants to keep going.

'You just read the rest of it, love,' says Delores, 'we're dying to see what happens.'

'Far away, on the edge of town someone has started a motor bicycle. Phut, phut. At first the sound is high and faint. But then it whirs like the buzz of bees. It could be the Rodriguez boys. More bees. Pistons. Engines. Where are they riding? My God, so close. More engines. Smoke from exhausts. The storks flap on their ledge. Men shade their eyes. Skin tightens on cheeks. Sun blazes. The traders strain to see, peering from below straw hats, but the Rodriguez boys do not arrive.

'The whine is sky birds and they are planes. No one moves at first. Metallic, the bell clangs. There are many bombs. A *niño* screams. Everyone runs, even the old, stumbling on sticks, but from the heavens, bullets rain in lines. Tearing the earth. Pam, pam. The chicks fall off their ledge. Also, the bullets rip people. Bombs drop on houses. Walls split and fall. Roofs collapse, and from the street, dust rises in quick little puffs. There is fire. A horse rears. "Murder," a woman cries, clutching her child.

'Miguel and Laura are the first to tumble.

'This, amigos,' says Therese, 'was a crime.'

It's the real deal. Her mask is vibrating. The wee gold stars flutter out and in as she breathes. A bomb is a bomb.

The silence inside the library is shouting.

Packie says something to her. His hand is on her arm. It's against the rules, but he doesn't care.

Out on the road, the cars head uphill to the carriageway, with strangers in them. None of themuns has heard the story. The purple Glider snakes in its lane, down to the city centre, with passengers sitting apart, as if nothing has happened, because nobody heard the screaming in Therese's story. The sound of the pain doesn't carry.

'This was humans killing humans, you understand,' she says. 'A crime of hate.'

'Fascists,' said the Englishman, 'Hitler and his old pal Franco, and the nationalists.'

'Do you know, to this day we are finding bits and bones?' Therese says. 'Last month, for example, someone discovered in the earth a brooch belonging to Señora Crux, who lost her legs. People still have no peace.'

The room is too hot now. Nobody knows what to say.

The drumming is louder. Blue lights are flashing. Sirens. An ambulance dashes. A cop car screeches.

'Give her a minute,' Packie says.

188

You want to say something. But you don't.

'Are you all right, Therese?' Pat says. 'I'm sure we all recognise the setting.'

I'm feeling bad for thinking about her and Packie.

'So emotional,' Pat says. 'Look at how Therese set the scene. How she pours herself into the story. How she transports us from lockdown here, in 2020, to Guernica over eighty years ago.'

Where was Guernica? I had to hand it to her. It was a true story.

'We're right there,' Pat says, 'and that's the secret. We're mingling with those ordinary, vulnerable people in the street.'

'It's so visual,' says Ruthie.

'God. And we know their names,' Delores says.

'I'm gutted,' says Cyril, the space man. He says what we're all thinking. That's how it was here, with our bombs and everything, and it's not that long ago. 'It could have been any of us,' he says. Nobody knows about my ma or Packie's.

'Mebbie somebody's ma was buying them trousers,' I say. 'Or a puppy for their birthday.' It was out of me before I knew.

'And where was God that day?' says Beth. People always ask that, but with her being good living and all, I was wondering… You never know. Maybe it was the wee fella. It was hard to say.

'I imagine that's what Picasso was thinking,' says Pat.

'It's very strong, darling,' says Delores.

I would have to ask Packie what the hell Picasso had to do with the nationalists? Was every country the same? Was there loyalists in Spain as well?

'Have you any thoughts, Packie?' Pat says, like he's the man.

'Yeah, I have,' Packie says – I want to catch his eye, but I don't – 'I have a lot of thoughts. It's desperate and marvellous and diabolical. It's wonderful writing, Therese. I'm completely floored.' He never said anything he didn't mean. I couldn't blame him for admiring her. I was moved myself.

'Are you able to tell us what happened to Miguel and his daughter?' Packie says.

'Miguel died,' she says. He gave… his blood. A sacrifice, you know. His daughter lived. Mi abuela. My grandmother.'

The whole room is feeling it.

'Would you like more time, Therese?' Pat asks.

Therese says something in Spanish. She looks at Packie. She says she'll be all right.

It wrecks me hearing it but I wouldn't have missed it. Writing is so bloody scary. It's an amazing thing, like something coming alive, or letting an animal out of a cage. It takes you by surprise. When you're not looking. A whole lot of times people say, 'This is only something I knocked out an hour ago,' but it's not true, because the next thing they're in tears. And so are you. Pat's dead right. The stuff comes out of your heart.

I'm sitting there thinking about my ma and all the things that happened after Cowdry's, when Pat says to me, 'Are you not going out for a smoke, Hooch?'

'Oh aye,' I say. It's the break. If there'd been no Covid we could have had a brew together in the wee squashed kitchen, and stood about yarning, with big mugs of coffee, talking, and eating Mikado biscuits out of the packet, like we used to. Now all we can do is go outside on our own and stand apart or sit six feet from each other on the concrete wall and look at the old prams and shopping trolleys that people dump in the Catwater. Nothing's the same. But then I'm thinking, maybe it's just as well, because how could you follow that there. And when everyone's affected as well as yourself, you never know how it will go. You can pick at a scab and start the bleeding all over again. But you can't keep it buried either.

So, I'm reaching for my Lamberts, on my own as I walk down the steps. A young fella in a wheelchair is playing a whistle on the corner. I give him a fag. 'You're a pal, mate,' he says. Packie has definitely got the hots for Therese and fair play to him. I keep telling myself not to worry about it, but I can't help it.

Just Published

Three years after you left me, one since you walked out of the world, and I've had ten treatments. Ten more to come. Not good. But I'm back on the train – not so much for the destination, I suppose, as for the sheer shunt of it.

The momentum.

To be on the move.

Between stations is mostly where I write.

Just get a publisher, you said.

A last command.

'You can't be any good, or you'd be speaking at Listowel,' a woman – presumably on the spectrum – told me once, over nibbles. I wondered if she was right.

The manuscript – I know, I know – still resting, doomed in darkness, or, alternatively, awaiting liberation? These days I'm into gentle workshops and competitions while I'm able.

Ah lighten up, you say. *Weren't you longlisted in the Penguin. Second in the bloody McManus?*

Consolation, but still the hanker. Not for me, but for the tale. I know you don't believe me.

Derry

Foyle glimmer. A sparkling-river morning. I've bagged a table on the seven thirty-eight. It's not the same since they welded the track. Gliding, no visceral clack. Sleek as a greyhound, the ThinkPad running on lithium. My hair grows back, thinnish, like a reseeded field, but visible. White egrets stalk.

Bellarena

This tiny station beyond Binevenagh's crag, reopened by Her Majesty, lost on peripheral platform, doughty in her green or red, as a tractor crossed the line.

Above, too high to even see, Lord Hervey's temple, a giant stone nipple. Years pass in sideglass window.

Refracted.

I'm facing myself now. Have to.

Smeared pale with factor 50, I'm an old man, who needs a woman, – can I say that – to keep him right. It's true. I'm wearing the Renoir hat.

Castlerock

The beach. The shorts you bought in TK Maxx. Don't worry, I'd never put them on. Not after all this time. And everything. Not now.

You left too soon.

Too soon?

I might have changed.

And Ulster might come to rest.

'Go for it,' the doctor said. 'You've got some time.'

I aim for the Christmas after next. I know that you don't hear this. You're done and dusted.

Slow down to cross the Bann.

Coleraine

Upstream they grab dead scrap and drop it into holds. I'm in the end carriage.

A cyclist, Rough Guide in hand.

Iron man and bike.

Remember the day you fell from yours in Normandie?

Ballymoney

Two rugby guys talk pints and pints.

Cullybackey

A bouncy girl in yellow cotton – I will say 'girl', she's under thirty – swings on. Her hessian bag spills novels. Big eyes, your eyes, the same deep violet.

'No shit,' she says.

'Oh yes,' I tell her. 'Three years ago.'

The books are 'work,' she says.

Climbed in beside me.

Of course, she did.

Without encouragement, as we used to say.

You used to say.

'Do you mind?' says the girl.

She knows I don't.

How bright she is.

'I write,' I say.

She smells of flowers. We both face front.

'Hate going backwards,' she says.

'Me too,' I say. 'Regrets, I've had a few.'

She hums the air. 'Ha, funding,' she says, 'I'm altogether skint.'

A hybrid accent. Her mother is from the west? The fringe.

Not straight.

The dress, definitely canary.

Her lips?

Ah yes. Her lips.

I might have known.

The heat. I shiver.

'Published?' she asks.

'Not yet,' I say.

Fifty years since New Jersey, staring at our reflections outside a store, the two of us; at beekeeper-men on the moon houses ablaze in Bombay Street.

Burned out.

I was.

I hear that train a coming. Forty wagons rolling south. I counted them one by one.

Ballymena

Her name?

Her name is Sam. She writes critiques. I smile.

'A private joke?'

I shake my head.

'A shift or two in "Bookends",' she says, 'beside the bank. Avoiding starvation by a wafer.' Muriel Spark, big time, if she gets the bursary.

If not?

'I'll sell my body.'

Her body?

No, really, she will.

'Terrific,' I growl.

Botanic

Already. Don't tell me the time flew in.

Two pavement beggars. I toss a quid and join the queue for coffee.

Young cardboard men in suits.

'To go?'… 'To go?'… 'What's yours?' … 'Sit in.'

Barista sunk deep in kohl. No sleep for nights.

I know the feeling.

Sam grabs a table. I buy hot chocolates.

'No mallows,' she says.

Like you.

No kidding.

No cream.

She smooths her dress, in that same old way. With two brown hands, cupping her mug, like a conspiracy. Below the table, I know she folds her legs.

She would.

On her feet, the espadrilles, they're black and white.

Size four?

What else?

I see.

The two of us. Heads coital.

Coital?

A turn of phrase. Astride the bentwood chairs.

Travelling back.

'What is it?' she asks.

'Memories,' I say. 'Bewleys.'

Ah, Bewleys.

She's never been to Dublin.

A lie, I'm sure.

'The National Gallery,' I say. 'Depending. You and me.'

An overnight. How stupid of me.

Columbian beans.

Get to the point.

Well, here it comes. Does this sound crazy? I put it to her.

Put what? You're so obtuse.

The plan to shift the manuscript.

What plan?

It seemed the thing to do, under the circumstances, for Sam and me.

For Sam and you?

Yes. Hocus pocus. A fairy tale.

'Why not?' Sam says. 'What is veracity?'

What indeed? What's in it for you?

A rocket launch.

A kind of union.

Another?

Of a spiritual nature. I order mochas.

Good man,' she says. 'What genre?'

You know what's next. 'Virginia W,' I say, 'it's niche, with a northern twist.'

Bloody Virginia. I might have guessed.

Cappuccino steam gurgles. Water – barista gulps a gallon. Wedges a window. Fag smoke and sirens.

'An orange stream of C?' she says. She stirs the dregs.

I understand. Of course I do.

Pink tongue, she licks her spoon. Back first. Convex. Concave.

Oh yes, I'm sure.

I know. How long ago in Quebec? Be honest.

Be honest?

I know.

'I see,' she says – she's quick like you. 'It's *Dalloway* with drums.'

'Kind of,' I say.

'Oh yum,' she says.

'You'll need the bathroom,' she tells me, before I feel the urge. With no edge to her voice.

If you're looking for sympathy…?

Same old familiar bladder business. But no excuses.

Excuses. My God.

'They keep the washrooms locked,' she says. 'You'll want the code. It's NEED2P.'

'That's good,' I say. 'I'll write it down.'

'Go on,' she says.

'Stay put,' I say.

'I'm a painted lady,' she tells me. 'I'll fly away.'

'Not yet,' I say.

How quaint.

No paper towels. I shake my arms, hands hanging, the way you grew to hate.

'Driers,' I say, 'they rip old skin.'

Skin rhymes with gin.

She'd been thinking – it hadn't taken long – about my proposal. I needn't spell it out.

I think you'd better.

Time's slackening bolt. All that.

Oh, fiddles, riddles.

I thought you'd see me through, you know, I never thought…

That's true. You never thought.

I somehow imagined… The Barista dabs with a milky cloth, to clean the spout. Attacking bent steel. Unclamping, tamping, grounds into the bucket they keep.

I should have gone after the first time, the second or third time.

'One shot or two?' Tears in the barista's eyes. Mascara melt, black purpling plum.

'Sit in?' she asks.

Tongs. Tongs. 'Too hard,' the croissants scream.

Always too hard.

'Will you stamp my card?' a young man asks.

'A commercial arrangement,' she says, 'that's all.'

Give me a break.

'I'm seventy, at least,' I say.

And age would stop you, then? There now, I've raised my voice.

'All right?' the barista signs to Sam.

'Okay.' Sam waves a hand. 'Age isn't a badge of honour,' she says to me.

I'm beginning to like the sound of her.

Her arm was asleep. Soft inside flesh. A rampant shoal of fish.

With tiny teeth.

Piranha, I'd say.

I asked.

You didn't.

'Could be,' she said.

And she'd never been to Dublin?

What did she think of fifty/fifty? I asked. Not that it mattered.

Go on.

'Eighty/twenty,' she said.

Eyes shining dollars.

Why should I care? 'Time's short,' I said. 'I'll be the unacknowledged ghost. You'll do the rest.'

I don't believe this.

'Events and all?' she said.

'Especially events. Appearances,' I said, 'chats; promotions. The whole damned caboodle. 'By December next year,' I said, you'll be discovered.'

A complete lie.

'No one wants an old guy,' I say.

You weren't always an old guy.

'You're young,' I told her, 'you have the jizz.'

'Oh lord,' she said, 'my Australian tutor loves my mind.'

What age is he?

'Does he?' I said, 'but will he back your book?'

'My book?' She liked the sound.

Her breath, your words.

'A deal,' I said.

'And what is our title?' she asked.

'Your title,' I told her. She wears Chanel.

'You married or what?' she asked.

Or what.

'I was,' I said.

'Ah yes,' she said, 'I see.'

She didn't.

'Brattled Brain.' I told her. 'That's what it's called.'

'Oh cool,' she said. 'A sleekit touch.'

Tide in. Tide out.

Remember the henna. Her hair's an autumn copper now and frizzy.

First lips. Now hair.

'How was it for the Aussie?' I asked.

'"Orgasmic" he said. "A novel kept hot inside my body."'

That's what he said?

And more. '"Raw as hell", he said. "A haemorrhage of the psyche."' God, prods – he's been here a while – '"and cerebellums, wrapped up like chips."' 'Normally,' she said, 'he would look for an agent, but he went straight to Pavorall.'

That's Pavorall and Sons?

Two Ls. That's right. Time's tight.

Five weeks before Christmas. Two thousand copies. *Brattles*, stands in piles. Sam's launch. Her signing. Mirror, mirror, I'm at the back, a ghost all right. Wedged between Nigella and the travel books.

'It's you.' A voice behind me. The autistic woman.

She points at Sam. 'Now there's a writer for you. One is never too old to learn. I'd take a leaf out of her book, if I were you.'

What pleasure does this give you?

The work is bigger than me.

God give me strength.

What might have been.

I rest each day at three. Did I tell you about Lynne Browne? Sam on her show.

Lynne from LA, she tries too hard…

'Joyce, for loyalists. I get it,' Lynne said, 'ha ha.'

'That's pigeonholing,' Sam said.

Well, good for her.

Sometimes Lynne gets it wrong.

Sometimes!

'A joke,' she said, 'in this city of pigeons.'

'And shit,' said Sam.

A family show.

I know.

'But seriously, as a point of reference…'

You couldn't write it.

I'm sitting under our Croatia snap. The one enamelled on the plate.

I thought you'd smashed it.

I'm sharing the space with a bee, unseasonal, ponderous, lost on my desk. I'm sipping whiskey.

'Joyce is your totem,' Sam said, 'not mine.'

She did?

Lynne cleared her throat.

The bee stays put. I pour another.

'Tell me,' said Lynne, 'how long were you… at the writing?'

'The book? Forever,' Sam said.

You and I were in high frost that sparking day in Crete. Five am before the gorge thawed. A wood fire, Americans, baggy and loud, warming their buns.

My husband will be a writer, you said, expressing confidence that one and only time.

Did I really?

Lynne tacked.

'But where have you been?' she said. You know, the way she does, 'I mean, it's just amazing.'

Boom boom.

'Your work has fledged and… well, we never knew. And what about your partner? What does she think?'

Sam has a partner?

I didn't know.

'She loves it,' Sam said, 'or so she tells me.'

It just gets better.

'An ageless quality,' Lynne said, 'and yet, so edgy.'

That must have pleased you.

Sam let her sweat.

Did Lynne hear 'Trilogy?'

Well, did she?

Can't say. 'It all depends,' she said.

Smart girl.

Sam's work was 'total – superlative,' Lynne said, in that gushy way she has. 'Now tell me truthfully, Sam, how much of this is actually you?'

You're making it up.

'A work of fiction,' Sam said. 'End of.'

How very true.

Lynne said she got it.

What a strange girl. And in espadrilles.

Some good reviews.

So, how do you feel?

I am both bigger and smaller, behind my father's desk, looking at the plaque they screwed to it, you know, for faithfulness.

You have a way with words.

The bee plods on.

'Page two hundred and sixty-five,' said Sam. She has a voice like yours. Clear, resonant, made for speaking out loud.

I sip and touch the bee. It's still alive.

A gentle finger.

A stranger's touch.

The slightest tremor.

Antennae tuned.

'By then,' Sam read, 'their wheels were turning. They began to spin apart, his revolving around himself, and hers tracing her own damned locus, both whirring in unconnected space, to a terrible, unsyncopated drum beat and with increasing velocity...'

The Long Spoon

It was a lazy, sunny afternoon. 'Grandpa, will you play a game with me?' Molly asked, all brightness in her cotton sunshine. 'It's a new one I've just invented. You won't have to run or jump, or even walk. All you have to do is sit back here in your special chair, among your roses, and I'll ask you some questions. It's called "Interview", is that all right?'

'Do I have a choice?' I asked.

'No,' she said, 'and you must give nice short answers or else you'll be disqualified.'

'Is there any cash in it?' I said.

'There's no actual money,' she said, 'but I'll bring you a can of Guinness from the fridge, to keep you happy. As long as you don't spill it over your fresh shirt when you pull the ring thingammy. It will be like a TV ad, kind of.'

'I wondered why you were all dressed up and looking so posh,' I said.

You are not to be asking me anything like that, even though you're dying to,' she said, 'and you have to stay polite and not argue.'

'Promise,' I said.

'I'll fetch your old straw hat, as well,' she said, 'in case you burn your head like you did last year, on sports day.' She skipped through the patio doors. Her broad red hairband was the same deep mahogany as the nasturtiums in the window boxes that came up every year, without any assistance from me. She was so like Felicity.

'Here we are then,' she said, all out of breath, hat in her right hand, beads of condensation slipping down the icy tin in her left. 'I'll bring you your beaker, too.' And off she scampered. What energy she had. 'Are you quite comfortable now?' she asked, settling me and holding up a spatula. 'This is the microphone,' she said, 'I want to talk to you about your bees. And remember, you mustn't be silly, like you sometimes are.'

'I'll have to work on my behaviour,' I said, tilting back the pewter tankard that Felicity brought back from Bavaria. I would stay in the now. The Guinness was good and today it beamed at me. 'That's a pint and a half, I'm telling you,' I said.

'First question,' she said. 'Do all the bees in a hive belong to one big family?'

'Ah now,' I said, swirling the widget in the light empty can.

'"Ah now," is no sort of answer,' she said.

'They all have the same mother,' I told her.

'Well, is she their queen?'

'Yes,' I said. 'She lays all the eggs.'

'Like a real mammy, in a way,' she said.

'She is a real mammy,' I said.

'I think that's being a little bit smart,' she said, raising her eyebrows. 'How many eggs does she lay?'

'A good queen lays hundreds of thousands in her lifetime,' I said. 'Most of them turn into female workers.'

'That would be a lot of daughters to look after,' she said, 'I mean, if they all hatched out. I'm sure you're glad there is just one granddaughter in this house. Are there any bad queens, like in fairy tales?'

'A healthy queen would have been a better way to put it,' I said. 'Sometimes they can be sick, you know, like you and me.'

'That wouldn't be their fault, though, would it?' she said. 'Human mammies get ill too, don't they, and they have to go to hospital. To Acacia One.'

'That's right,' I said, seeing Felicity's wan face. 'They do indeed.'

'What are the daddies like?' asked Molly.

'The drones? There are only a few hundreds of them. They're fatter than the workers, with big, blunt backsides. Six or seven drones will mate with one queen, so most of the new little bees will be half-sisters.'

'Like me and Lucy,' she said.

Lucy was eighteen when she left for Glasgow. Oh God.

'She used to tell me stuff about her daddy. I hope she's not in hospital,' Molly said.

'Maybe we'll see her again sometime,' I said.

'I say a prayer every night for her,' she said.

'I'm sure that will help,' I said. My throat was parched. I took another draught.

'Don't wipe your mouth with the back of your hand like that,' she said. 'Honestly, I'll get you a tissue.' Felicity was right there, looking at me.

'Apologies, viewers,' she said, back in her role, 'this is a very old beekeeper. Do bees live in happy families?' she asked, in her best presenter's voice.

'We can't speak of them being happy or unhappy,' I said. 'Perhaps content comes closer.'

'So, they are not like us,' she said.

I must have smiled.

'What's funny?' she said.

'They don't have feelings, like we do,' I said. 'They have been programmed for millions of years by evolution.'

'Now another thing,' she said, 'can you tell me if they have any enemies inside the hive? You know, or things that would do them harm, because our audience will want to know.'

'Oh yes,' I said.

'Like what?' she said.

'Like diseases and intruders. We can put on mouse guards, but parasites are a big problem,' I told her. 'You always get parasites. They are...'

'I'm sure we all know what parasites are,' she said, waving the spatula. 'They live off other creatures. We learned about them in school. Mammy used to say that Joe was one.'

'One what?'

'A parasite.'

'There's a particular pest that attacks bees,' I said, 'by clinging to the hairs of their bodies and legs and sucking them dry.'

'That's awful,' she said. 'Would Mammy and I be dead if the police hadn't taken him away?' Why did she want him to be my daddy anyway?'

'She wasn't herself,' I said.

'Will he ever get out of jail?' she asked.

'It will be a very long time,' I said. 'You'll be quite grown up by then.'

'But what I want to know,' she said, 'is, are there no kind drones to be good to the queen and to stand up for her babies?'

'It's not in their nature, they're not like people,' I said.

'Hmmm,' she said. 'Emily Robinson and her sister Amy said it was all the daddies in their house that got them into trouble. They had to go into foster care.'

'That must have been tough for them,' I said.

'Do the drones ever... hurt the queen?' she asked.

'Why do you ask?' I said. For a moment I saw her hesitate. Then she flicked her hair. 'I'm asking the questions,' she said.

'Oops, I forgot,' I said. 'No, the drones die after they mate with the queen and that is the end of them.'

'Even so,' she said, 'I love to think of a gigantic rubbish heap of drones. I hate them so much. We should make a fire in a bucket and burn their bodies.'

'A kind of insect crematorium,' I said.

'That's right,' she said. 'For drones.'

'But then the bees would die out,' I said.

'I don't care,' she said. 'Do you think bees have long memories?'

'They can remember enough to get back to their own hives,' I said, 'but if the weather's wet and they're not flying they can become confused and then they need to memorise the landmarks all over again.'

'I was at five different schools in seven years,' she said. 'Lucy told me she remembered things happening to Mammy in West Park. She said the inside of her own head was like a dead bird she saw squashed on the street. All bloody and stinky.'

'She had a rough time,' I said. 'You all did. Felicity was poorly long before you lived with me.'

'Lucy said there was no one looking after us. Only bad people.'

'Mental illness puts a big strain on a family,' I said. 'It should have been easier when you all moved up closer, but your mammy wanted to do everything for you two by herself.'

'And then I came to be with you,' she said in her firm little voice. 'So, who is there to protect the bees?'

'Bee sentinels,' I said.

'Actual bees?'

'Yes, real bees on duty. Tomorrow you can put on the small bee suit we got from Thornes and watch them patrolling the entrances to the hives.'

'Like good soldiers,' she said. 'I think that's brilliant. But, Grandpa, sometimes I dream about monsters in glasses with thick dark rims. I think they must look like drones.' Her lip was trembling. 'Oh well,' she said. 'I suppose an interviewer isn't supposed to talk about herself.'

'Interviewing is a tricky business,' I said. 'A good correspondent will be emotional underneath. It's how she makes sense of things. She can't help being affected.' I tapped on the empty can.

'That sounds like the Test Match tune,' she said. 'Do you want another one?'

'To keep the vocal cords vibrating,' I said. 'And bring yourself a Loop the Loop.'

'That will be all on bees for this week, viewers,' she said, suddenly remembering the spatula. 'It's nearly all over,' she whispered. 'There are just a couple of extra questions I want to ask without the cameras. Now don't fall asleep.'

'Here we go,' she sang, skipping back along the crazy paving and handing me the can, 'reinforcements. I'll have the ice pop when we're really finished. I want to ask you one last thing.'

'Ask away,' I said.

'It's kind of hard to find the right words,' she said, jiggling her leg.

'Try,' I said.

'Well,' she said, with all Felicity's earnestness as a child, 'do you think it might have been better if I had been born, you know, into the world of bees? Instead.'

'Instead of being a human baby?'

'Yes,' she said. 'Like a grub.'

'May I break the rules?' I said.

'It's okay. There's only the two of us now,' she said.

'What would you say yourself,' I said, 'if I were to ask you?'

She stared at two bees on the snapdragons for what seemed like a long time. 'I think it could have been better in some ways,' she said, with her head to the side. 'For instance, I liked hearing about the queen laying the eggs. And I suppose an insect couldn't lie in bed all day and get depressed or cry and drink too much.'

'I can see that,' I said.

'I would definitely want to see the guard bees doing their job, to keep out the invaders, but on the other hand, bee drones can't do you any harm. So, I suppose that would be all right. You see,' she said, looking right into my soul, 'I keep all my bad memories in an old suitcase in my head, like the one Mammy has, and sometimes I'm scared it will burst open, and they will all come crawling out, like maggots. Even ones I didn't know were in there.'

'I'm sorry,' I said.

'I bet a bee would have forgotten all about them,' she said. 'The creatures are like giant insects in my dreams, trying to climb through my windows and there are no guards. I keep thinking they are coming for me with their big jaws, and I am in Acacia One.'

'Would you rather not visit your mammy for a while?' I asked. 'She doesn't want you to be frightened. I wouldn't make you go, you know.'

Molly sat on the wicker chair beside me and slipped her hand into my old man's paw. 'Your arms are so brown,' she said, 'but you should put on sun block the same as me. Tory Conroy, this girl I know, says her grandpa was a terrible old grump, but she cried when he died of skin cancer.'

'I'll buy a tube in Boots,' I said.

A cloud had obscured the sun.

'Is seventy-five so very old?' she asked.

'Not these days,' I said. 'My dad was over ninety when he died. You can give me a call at night,' I said. 'I'm never far away. I don't sleep well, so I'll hear you, no matter what time it is.'

'They're away by the morning,' she said, 'and then I can put them out of my head, because when I wake, I'm glad to be here in my own room, with the light shining through the primrose curtains and with Patch licking my face. And then I hear you downstairs bumbling around and making the porridge.'

'Bumbling, is that what I do?'

'And there's honey and pancakes for breakfast and it feels like I've always been here. Do you understand?'

'I think so,' I said, stretching out my arms.

'Just be patient,' she said. 'I'll give you a hug in a minute. I want to tell you one last secret that nobody knows.'

'Oh yes,' I asked, 'what's that?'

'I'm going to become a beekeeper, like you,' she said.

'An assistant at last,' I said. 'That's the best news I've heard today.'

'Only today?' she said. 'How do I get started?'

'Well, tomorrow we'll take a walk over to see Wendy in the association and see about getting you a smart box of bees and a little queen of your own.'

The cloud had lifted.

'Of course, I know it will take years for me to know as much as you,' she said.

'The thing is, when you keep bees, you are always learning,' I said. 'Every single day. Beekeeping is like life. It has many ups and downs. Sometimes you are not sure why something happens.'

'I'll stick with it,' she said. 'I was just thinking, that even if Mammy and Lucy don't come back for ages, when they do, I'll be twirling the long spoon you brought me from Scotland, into a jar of my very own honey, and they'll love it on their toast.'

'You are a great girl, Molly,' I said. 'It's going to be such an adventure.'

Woman Calling

When I was a child, 'visiting' was a thing. In a way, it was more demanding for us as kids than having people to our home, requiring more face shimmer and formality. I wore my square boys' jacket, short pants, striped narrow tie. My sister's shoes gleamed jasper against blue whitener socks.

Trotted out, hair shining like ponies, we were docile reflections of our parents, admired, no doubt, for our head-to-the-side Sunday manners and good skin, by friends and relatives.

We bumped up tracks in the bull-nosed Morris, to broken-down farms, stood in low slung byres to watch the milking; big patient cows having their udders tugged, suds floating warmly in pails. Once, a bullock on a tether swung an ancient cousin around a paddock in a mad romp. All faecal clabber. He waved as they sailed past.

On other jaunts, if it didn't lash, we'd stroll around some riddled garden to admire the dahlias or be astounded by the plumpness of leeks, tread carefully a green baize lawn or listen to an ancient couple sing duets. Once, on a mossy tennis court, we wobbled on a motorised bicycle. Mostly, we were lucky if there was a cat to pet or an elderly one-eyed dog.

One of these trips led us to the dark, terraced house of Mr Toffee, a translucent gentleman of maybe eighty, and his tiny wife. They had befriended my parents during the war, and other courting couples who didn't go to bars, laying on Easter treasure hunts in the expansive grounds of their red-roofed bungalow at Millisle, which they remembered as a pleasant place. There had been picnic spreads and fellowship, singing in harmony, home baking and harmless ginger pop.

Mr Toffee was an artist. We owned two of his early works. The one I liked depicts Irish cottages, gable turf stacks, and a blue expanse of water. In the foreground, a countrywoman, splashed red in petticoats, calls to her neighbour across an unpaved street. Grass tufts wild on sand. You see a yellow beach, the rising hills beyond, a big sky and a single sailboat on the lough.

But the Toffees had sold their bungalow. This house was dull and cramped.

Family visiting often involved a polite hanging about. Time to study a glazed plaque from Aberystwyth, a wedge of flying mallards, the ibex horn brought back by missionaries, from Uganda, embroidered texts. 'The unseen Guest at every meal.'

Mrs Toffee melted into the scullery. She closed the door. Smiling, Mr Toffee shrugged. He joined her. There would be tea. We sat into their rounded, wooden-armed settees – and chatted in the muted way of scrubbed families talking together on a bus, or at a wake, conscious of being overheard, aware that the Toffees could be on us at any moment.

My mother sparkled. There was a dancing, edge-of-the-seat, conspiracy life about her eyes, but no harm in the trill of her mouth, on the upturned tip of her nose. The longer we sat, the more tremulous her stage whisper, though, the more tinkly and elastic her laugh. 'Dear love them,' she said, at last, squeezing my knee too hard, 'they've got very old.'

The Toffees were fussing. You could hear their muffled scolding, the sporadic clink of occasional china being lifted from shelves. My mother knocked, offering help.

'Not at all, dear,' they chorused, two worn-out heads appearing around the door jamb at different heights. The very idea. A kettle sang, reaching a covert crescendo more than once. Somewhere a clock chimed – bong. The door half-opened. False start. More murmuring. The Toffees in conference. My mother rolling her eyes.

What a lark it all was, before the balloon fizzled and the fun went out of it.

Mrs Toffee toddled in bearing a tilted tray, scolding her white-haired husband. Where were the linen napkins, the stand to set the teapot on? We chewed bought cake and dry currant squares. She was all fumble and spoons. It was about the mechanics. The production. The handing out of plates. The rattling of cups. Two sugars or one? Did they even get around to the memories of the blitz and the great times they'd had together?

When she poured, Mrs Toffee's doll hands shook. Mr Toffee hovered, transparent as a ghost, calling her 'Mammy', though they'd never had children. 'She finds it hard to see,' he said. 'Her cataracts are bad.'

'We manage,' she said.

There were sighs. Perhaps that's when I learned to pause. To keep quiet when there was nothing to say.

'No painting, no.' His long brushes stayed dry these days. There was no room for his mess of pots and palette. 'Between collecting prescriptions and going for pints of milk, I've a full-time job. Och aye,' he said, holding out freckled hands, 'all that is over.'

Mrs Toffee trembled.

'The tea was lovely,' we told her, like we'd been taught.

There were tears in my mother's eyes.

In the end she too would shamble around her kitchen, pacemaker ticking silently inside her, leaning often on grey worktops to catch a breath, eye-bright as ever and curious, but not hearing what we said and taking forever at nothing.

I am seventy-one now. Mr Toffee's painting hangs above my desk. The same smoke wafting from the cottage chimneys. The thatch remains intact, waves ripple. The sail boat tacks. Clouds cast a shadow I'd never noticed until recently. The woman in petticoats stands on the same spot, still calling.